PIECES OF ME

Shiloh Walker

Copyright

Initial Copyright © 2017 Shiloh Walker

Cover: Shiloh Walker
Image: Anastasia_vish | Bigstock
Cover Text & Design: Picmonkey
Editing by Pamela Campbell & Kathryn Flaherty

To my editor, Pam…loved working with you again. To Kathryn, who put her things aside to work on this.

To all the women who've had to fight monsters. You're stronger than you know.

To my family. Always. I thank God for you.

CHAPTER ONE

I woke with a scream echoing in my ears.

It was one a.m. but the lights shone, bright as day, in my room.

Being in the dark was enough to terrify me. Cowering in the middle of my bed, I drew my knees to my chest and shivered.

"I'm free." I drew in a breath, let it out. "I'm free."

The sound of my voice grounded me, a little.

"I'm free."

It took several minutes of breathing, of talking to myself before I no longer felt as if the nightmare was going to overwhelm me. Longer still before I was willing to uncurl from the protective ball I'd curled into as the echoes of the dream washed over me.

I got out, I told myself. *I got away. He doesn't control me anymore. I'm not just a thing.*

Carefully, feeling like I might break, I got out of bed and padded into the bathroom.

"You're you," I said. My voice was rougher than it had once been, husky. A guy at a bar had told me it was sexy as fucking hell—those had been his words.

I wish I could appreciate the compliment. But my sexy-as-fucking-hell voice had happened because I'd spent too much time *trapped* in a very real hell and I'd screamed until I'd damaged my vocal cords.

Hard to appreciate having a phone-sex kind of voice when that's what it took to get it.

Still, at least I can talk now. I stared at my pale reflection and spoke again. "You're you. You're Shadow. And you got away."

I was no longer the nothing, the nobody he'd made me. I was no longer just a silent scream in the dark, and that was what mattered.

Because the dregs of the dream still clung to me, I stripped out of my clothes and climbed into the shower, turning the water on as hot as I could tolerate. Standing under the spray until the water started to chill, I let it wash away the stain of the dream as I continued my morning mantra.

I'm me. I can leave my home. I can go shopping. I can go to the beach.

"He isn't here to stop me."

Outside, the sun was starting to edge up over the horizon and the fist of terror began to ease. Daytime was always better. I was too old to be afraid of the dark, but I wasn't going to feel shame over that small thing.

I had too many other things to be ashamed of.

Wrapping a towel around myself, I used another to dry my hair and moved to stand in front of the mirror. The reflection staring back at me looked like an urchin—a wet, bedraggled one.

I turned away from the reflection and grabbed my robe. I'd get coffee. I'd get to work. I'd make myself forget...for a little while.

And I'd pretend it was enough.

It wouldn't be, though.

Nothing was ever enough.

▲▼▲

There are times in my life when I look back over the years and it's as if I'm watching a film of somebody else's life.

My life seemed to stop when I was twenty. It just...stopped and some other stranger took over. It wouldn't surprise me to see a headstone, complete with my name.

Here lies Shadow Grace Harper...her life stopped at age 20.

My name truly is Shadow. My mother loved the TV show *Dark Shadows*, but the name Barnabas didn't really suit a baby girl and none of the female cast had really appealed. But she liked Shadow Grace and my dad indulged her. Always.

He indulged her, spoiled me. Then, when I was sixteen, they both left me, stolen in a car crash when a tired truck driver fell asleep at the wheel.

I was sent to live with an aunt who barely tolerated my existence.

It wasn't all that terribly bad. I didn't like her, she didn't like me, but we managed to coexist right up until I turned eighteen. Then I left that tired, gray house behind, heading for the quiet, bucolic charm of Pawley's Island, South Carolina, buying one of the charming old mansions and settling in for what I'd hoped to be the life of an artist.

Life changed a few months later when I realized so many of the kids my age were going off to school. It was too late for me to try to get in anywhere, so I'd spent that year having fun and doing all the things I hadn't been able to do with my aunt, while getting ready to start college a bit later.

At nineteen, I started college—attending the University of Massachusetts. I kept the Pawley's Island house, letting a realtor talk me into renting it out as a vacation property while I was in school, because sooner or later, I'd come back there. I loved Pawley's Island, loved the laziness of the place, loved the sunrises on the beach, the people. Everything about it, really.

But I had college to worry about and my plans had been to pursue... something artsy.

That had been my plan. Something artsy.

At nineteen, with more money than sense, it had been a viable goal in my mind. I'd get a degree and maybe I'd spend my life painting or teaching. Or maybe I'd just find a way to be happy.

Could that be a life's goal? A job? Being *happy*? Finding a way not to be lonely, the way I had been ever since my parents died?

I didn't know. I no longer understood that girl, but then again, she died a long time ago.

It was at UMass that I met and fell in love with a handsome, sophisticated older man. I was twenty when I met Stefan Stockman. He was fifteen years older than me and he was the beginning of the end for the girl I'd been—that silly, foolish Shadow Grace Harper. After a whirlwind courtship that lasted less than six months, we married.

I hadn't even turned twenty-one.

We were still on our honeymoon when the change started. It was slow, it was subtle...and it was terrifying. Shadow wasn't a suitable name for his wife, so naturally I became Grace. The loud, boisterous laugh wasn't suitable, so naturally, I learned to laugh quietly, behind my hand...and then I just stopped laughing at all.

Naturally. It all happened naturally.

And naturally, in my mind, it's easier to view it all as something that just happened to somebody else. As a movie. Something that I can view as just somebody's bad dream, not something that happened to me.

The movie ended when I was twenty-five and I woke up in the hospital, just a few short hours after I stumbled out of the basement of a house

I didn't recognize, freed, oddly enough, by a freak tornado that had killed eight people. It killed eight people, but it saved me.

Yet another thing to be ashamed of—the storm killed eight people, shattered the lives of others.

But it freed me. I was so pathetically grateful for it.

Sitting at the table, lost in memories, I sketched, unaware of what I was even drawing until I was done.

When I finished, I found myself staring at a picture of me—my own face. Only it wasn't *right*. My face no longer looked like my own, yet another sign of how completely gone that girl was.

After spending months in hell, after being beaten multiple times, plastic surgery had been required to fix the damage. My right cheekbone had been broken and healed badly. Swelling and an infection inside my sinuses had required another surgery, and my nose, also the recipient of several hard blows, needed repair as well.

The last beating had fractured my jaw and I had scars on my body.

I don't even know where many of the scars came from.

Memories of those months are vague and some are gone completely.

That is another thing I am grateful for—I don't want to remember *any* of that time. Even losing a few memories is a blessing.

I studied my altered face and the dream came back to me.

I'd tried to leave.

That was what had set him off.

I'd tried to leave and he came after me, dragged me back…and practically threw me away, locking me away someplace so dark, so desolate, nobody had even heard my screams.

The phone rang, making me jump.

"Hello."

"Hello, darling."

I smiled at the sound of his voice. Only Seth could call me and immediately make me smile. "You better not flirt with me. Marla will get jealous."

"Marla is standing right here. And she says 'hi, honey'." Seth imitated his girlfriend's New Jersey accent almost perfectly, drawing another smile from me.

"Tell her I said 'hi' back. What are you up to?"

"We're driving up to Myrtle Beach tonight…going to hit a bar or two, get drunk. Ride the Ferris wheel. Come with."

A pang of longing went through me. "No."

"Come on, babe…come with us. Have fun. We'll go to the beach."

"I can go to the beach here and it's a lot quieter. Also, there was another shark sighting near Myrtle Beach. I don't think so." Sharks weren't what scared me. I'd faced much worse things than sharks. But I wasn't going to tell him that I couldn't handle being in a crowd, unaware of who could be there, who might be watching me.

"If any sharks come near you, I'll chase them off," he promised.

"No, Seth."

He sighed. "Sooner or later, I'm going to get you off Pawley's Island. You need to learn to have fun again, babe."

"I do have fun. Every other Thursday, for movie night."

We chatted for a few more minutes and agreed on a movie for the following day—Thursday, movie night—and then he hung up. After I lowered the phone back to the table, I reached out and traced a finger down the line of my sketched, slightly imperfect jaw.

I wished I had the courage to go with him.

I wished I wasn't so afraid.

But my ex-husband was still out there.

And worse…he knew where I lived.

▲▼▲

I sat at the table and looked outside.

When I saw the man sitting on the steps of the house diagonal to mine, I eased back and tried to pretend I hadn't seen him.

He'd seen me, though. I knew he had. After all, he was being paid to sit there and watch and wait. Paid to spy on me.

It was like having my ex-husband there, staring at me, watching me.

A silent reminder. *You'll never be free of me…*

I ran away from him once, but he just found another way to torment me. That fear of him still haunts me, controls me. *He* still haunts me, controls me.

He still watches me and I know it, even though I left Boston and moved back to Pawley's Island. I had money…a lot of it. A fact that probably pissed off my ex-husband. If he could have controlled that money, he could have maybe controlled me, kept me from leaving.

The money was from my parents, a trust fund that had been left for me after their deaths. He was rich himself, but the money I'd inherited once I turned twenty-five made his net worth look…paltry. He hadn't realized that I'd only get yearly lump sums until I was twenty-five. Then I'd receive the bulk of it.

I'd foolishly let him know about the inheritance that would be mine, but he hadn't clued into the deal about the lump sums until later.

If I could figure out how to do it, maybe that money would buy my freedom. Sometimes I fantasized about trying to hire somebody to kill him, but I never followed through.

Other times I thought about buying myself a new life somewhere, a new name.

I had the money.

I'd researched how.

I might even work up the courage to do it.

Nibbling on my thumbnail, I stared around the edge of the curtain at the man paid to spy on me. He sipped his coffee and stared back. It didn't even seem to bother him that he was making my life hell.

Turning my back on him, I shut him out of my mind. At least I tried.

"Find something else to do," I told myself. Find another way to get back at him—not the man on the porch. But *him*. My ex-husband. The man who still sought to control me.

Almost everything I did was some sort of small, subtle rebellion.

Coming back to Pawley's Island, cutting my hair, even the clothes I wore.

I was running out of new ideas, but even walking barefoot to the beach that was just beyond my porch was something that would have made him furious. That was what I would do, I decided. I'd go to the beach.

▲▼▲

I'd pulled on a long flowing skirt and a tank top. Another one of my small rebellions. I looked like a modern day hippy, my short, choppy hair already disheveled from the ever-present breeze. I'd tied a bandana around my wrist. Once I settled down to work on my sketches, I'd need it to keep my hair back, but for now, I loved the feel of the wind.

With my bag over my shoulder, I headed out the back door. I didn't know how long it would take my shadow to find me. Sooner or later, when I didn't show up through a window, he'd come looking, but for a little while, I was untethered.

There was coffee in a thermos and I munched on toast as I walked. Gulls circled overhead and a few came down to land close by, hoping I'd toss down my meager breakfast. They could hope as much as they wanted. They weren't getting my toast.

My phone beeped just as I reached the table at the very edge of my property, right before it gave way to sand. It wasn't quite ten but others were already hitting the beach and as I pulled out my phone, I studied everybody, distrust as much a part of me as the color of my eyes.

After I'd assured myself that none of them were my ex, I looked at my phone screen. Instinctively, a smile curled my lips.

It was Seth, or rather a picture.

He and Marla were standing by one of the kiosks that rented out movies and he was pretending to gag himself while Marla fanned herself with the chosen movie.

I laughed and texted him back.

Don't watch it without me.

The best thing that had happened since I'd left Boston had been meeting Seth, the hottest, most intense man I'd ever met. When he knocked on my door, he'd terrified me. He'd been with another equally hot man—his lover at the time—and I'd been so scared I'd barely been able to vocalize two words.

They'd known it, too.

But Seth had refused to leave, insisting that he had something important to tell me. In the end, he'd asked if I could at least meet him at the little coffee shop in town.

I'd agreed.

He'd told me that I had to promise to be there, otherwise, he'd just come back and knock, and sing very badly, until I agreed to talk to him.

I've learned over the years that Seth does sing very badly indeed.

I also learned that his lover, Tony, would have been just fine if I hadn't met them at the coffee shop.

Seth, though, was a tattooed, tarnished knight, always looking for somebody in distress.

He had a record—petty theft and other issues that had landed him in jail for a year—but he was trying to turn his life around, going to school, paying bills. He explained all of that upfront, while I sat there, confused and not quite following. Then he told me that my ex-husband had approached him.

The pieces clicked and fell together as he explained that my ex had tried to bribe him to watch me.

He lived in the house just across from mine and it would have been a perfect plan, except Seth wasn't an asshole.

My heart had knocked against my ribs the entire time and I'd waited, terrified of what he was going to say, even though a part of me already knew. I'd already seen one of the neighbors who was either really into fruit, or just too fixated on me, because he showed up every time I was at the fruit stand to buy more mangos for the smoothies I'd gotten addicted to.

My ex-husband was having people watch me.

Seth had been willing to testify. We called the cops.

Cops came by to talk to Seth a few days later, then drove off.

When I asked him what happened, he refused to tell me.

But I knew it had something to do with my ex.

I'm surprised Seth's still my friend.

Tony isn't. They fought for weeks and less than three months after that, Tony moved out.

He met Marla a few months later and they've been together ever since. I think he's seriously in love with her. He had grinned at me when I saw them together and told me, "I never did see the point in tying myself down on anything. I go both ways."

It had made me laugh, even as I wished I could be more like that. I do nothing but tie myself down. To my fear, to the memories. To my husband's controlling nature.

All of it controls me, even now, nearly three years after a storm freed me from hell.

I'd gone back to college, but I never did pursue being an art teacher. That was what I'd wanted…well, before. There was no way I could stand that now. People would watch me. Want to talk to me. Ask me questions.

I went into graphic design instead and that was better. I could work from my home. I was safe there. Safe inside those walls, where he couldn't watch me. Where he couldn't spy.

Where I was alone.

But sometimes…being alone is just too much.

Sometimes, being alone just sucks.

Too often, I still feel as though I'm trapped in some awful nightmare.

I'm so desperately ready to wake up.

Sighing, I settled down at my favorite table and took a sip of my coffee. The water was rough today. It matched my mood and I closed my eyes, letting the sound of the waves crashing against the beach soothe me.

The hours passed by too fast, yet it was a slow, almost pleasant crawl. I was blissfully aware of the sun on my back, the wind in my hair.

And him.

There was another reason I loved coming to the beach.

Another reason I liked sitting there.

I don't know his name. He's at the beach almost as often as I am and if he's ever noticed me staring at him, he hasn't given any sign. So I let myself stare and I let myself watch. I let myself wish.

Sometimes, just looking at him makes me hurt inside. It's a pins-and-needles sort of feeling, as if something in me is trying to come back to life—slow, painful life.

I watch him and I think about what it would be like if I had the courage to go up to him and say *hi*.

If I had the courage.

But he was the kind of man who was forever out of my reach.

It was safer that way, too. He was larger than life, full of heat and energy and a raw kind of masculine beauty that made the body go almost numb.

He was too intense. Too big. Too there. And he had a way about him that made me think he could be cruel. He had a wolf tattooed across his back and since I didn't know his name, I called him Lobo.

Big, dark and built, he looked like he belonged to the beach. Or maybe the beach belonged to him. His hair was so short, it looked like he buzzed it off with a razor every day when he rolled out of bed. Thoughts of him and bed made my heart jump around inside my chest and needs I'd forgotten I even had stirred inside me.

There was a tattoo over his left pectoral—a vivid starburst—although I'd never been close enough to see the details too clearly. On his back was that wolf. A massive, snarling wolf. It started low on his spine, stretched up across the elegant, ridged muscles and finished with the wolf's muzzle around his left shoulder.

Maybe Lobo seemed an odd name for him, but he stalked the beach like a predator and I needed to have some name for him since I couldn't just think *him* every time I saw him, thought of him. Dreamed of him.

And I did dream about Lobo.

The dreams about him were the only respite I had from my nightmares. Hot and sweaty dreams, the kind I'd never thought I'd have again. Torrid, dirty dreams that had me moaning and clenching my thighs together, longing to touch…and be touched.

Dreams that had me waking feeling empty, filled with longing.

Wishing I was anybody but who I was.

Wishing I had the courage to reach out and take what I wanted, what I needed.

And I so desperately needed.

My skin prickled and I looked up as his gaze casually brushed over me. Our gazes collided and my breath caught in my throat before I looked back down, staring at the sketch in front of me.

It was Lobo again.

He was naked...again.

My favorite way to portray men.

It wasn't always sexual, but lately, that was how I did it. I couldn't find any other means of satisfaction and I didn't see that changing. The fear inside me was too great. It wasn't that I feared sex, exactly.

After the first hellish year of my marriage, my husband had stopped wanting *sex* with me. He might force me, but sex, lovemaking...the intimacy, all of that had ceased.

He used to taunt me with it, because I think he knew I'd wanted it. Not necessarily with him, but...just sex. The connection. The intimacy. The feel of a body pressed against mine. I'd wanted to be wanted. But he'd denied me that. Even as he'd battered me in every other way imaginable.

There were nights when I'd wake up with my face shoved into the pillow while he tore into me and I'd bite my lip bloody to keep from crying. When it was over, he'd tell me about the whores, his mistress, even how he had more pleasure just jacking off in the shower—all things that were better at getting him off than me.

And to think I'd thought that was hell. That was nothing. That was easy. I hadn't really known hell until—

My mind shied away. I couldn't think about the final months.

I didn't *want* to, either.

I wanted to think about here...about now.

The beach, the sun shining down on my back, so hot and intense, the wind teasing at my hair, the rhythmic lull of the ocean as the waves crashed into the sand. Voices...always voices. I craved the sound of people now, even if I didn't know them.

Just as I craved the light, the feel of the sun shining down on me, and the sight of people. Old, young, unattractive, or so beautiful they made the heart sigh. It didn't matter.

Right now, though, I was sketching the one who made *my* heart sigh and my body yearn.

Sketching out the image of the man. Lobo...the focus of all the hot and crazy dreams. The only focus. The relief from my nightmares.

This sketch was a bad one to be doing here.

He was standing, his back braced against a wooden post, the sand under his feet, waves washing up around him. And his hands were fisted in my hair. I was on my knees in front of him, fully dressed, while I took his cock into my mouth.

Drawing it was the most arousing sort of foreplay, and the most frustrating, because there would be no end, no way to fulfill this aching hunger. Heat gathered in me as I imagined taking that cock inside my mouth, wondering how close I was to *really* capturing how he would look naked. A pulse of hunger throbbed deep inside me and I bit my lip to stifle a groan as I imagined how his hands might tighten to urge me on.

He wouldn't be a gentle lover.

I don't think I *needed* a gentle lover.

What I needed, what I *craved*, was a lover, period.

Somebody who wanted me. Needed me.

My face was flushed and hot as I finally finished the sketch. I was going to embarrass myself if I tried another one like that out here. Embarrass myself or just leave myself too shaky to make the walk back home. Unless I took a plunge into the waves crashing against the beach.

I flipped to a fresh sheet of paper and started a new sketch.

His hands this time. Just his hands.

They fascinated me. Long fingers, broad palms.

Were his hands rough? How would they feel rasping—

"Watch out!"

I flinched and cowered, instinctively curling in on myself and not even a second later, pain licked across my cheekbone, spreading up. Numbness hit a second after that and the fear, always hidden so close under the surface, crept out.

The football lay on the ground next to me and I stared at it, my eyes tearing as my head started to ache and pound.

The familiar wisp-wisp-wisp of footsteps falling across the sand caught my attention and I jerked my head up, watching as two of the college boys who liked to hang out at the beach came running toward me.

"Hey, are you okay?"

The haze of confusion started to clear and I pieced together what had happened. He wasn't here—my ex. He hadn't found me. Hadn't hit me. I wasn't in danger. It was a football. It had hit me. I was okay. My head hurt and my face hurt, but I was okay. I'd taken so much worse.

"Ma'am?"

The sound of that worried voice almost shattered me and I realized it didn't matter if my ex-husband wasn't here. I was going to fall apart soon.

I jerked my head around and started to gather up my supplies.

Leave. I had to leave.

A hand touched my shoulder and I jerked back, falling on my ass onto the sand.

Now, the slow, hot rush of blood started to creep up my cheeks and those two boys stood over me, watching me. One had a smirk on his face and he didn't bother to hide it. The other looked bewildered. "I just wanted to make sure you're okay," he said, lifting one hand and then letting it fall helplessly to his side. "You...your face is red."

"Leave the freak alone, Tony," his friend said, nudging him in the shoulder. "She looks like she's going to scream rape all because you touched her. Come on, let's—"

The kid turned and stopped in his tracks.

I stopped as well, my breath frozen, everything in me frozen, as horror slammed into me.

He was there, too. Just a few feet away and he had a grim look on his face.

Lobo. Whatever his name was.

"Ah...hey, Jinx." The long, lanky college kid guy smiled, but even despite my fear, I could see the strain on his face. "How are you?"

Jinx? His name was Jinx? Or maybe it was short...for...for something. Staring at my knees, I tried to get my legs underneath me so I could move, get to my feet, get away. But my limbs were frozen. *I* was frozen, all but locked in place with shock and fear and horror. *Get away. Get away.*

I tried so hard to deal with the panic attacks. But sometimes, they crept out to bite me in the ass, and this one was so close I could already feel its teeth.

"How am I?" Lobo asked, his face drawn tight as he took a step toward the kid who'd been mocking me. "You don't want to ask. You pull a shit thing like that and then be an asshole about it? Get the fuck out of here."

As they got the fuck out of there, the fear that had frozen me finally loosed its grip and I was able to move. Needed to get out of there. I felt exposed.

So exposed, kneeling on the sand to pick up my sketch pad. The sketch I'd just drawn was right there and I hurriedly snapped the book shut. A blush scalded my cheeks red as I turned and snatched up my charcoal pencils, the eraser, everything I'd dropped as fast as I could. As I reached for one of my smaller sketchbooks, a shadow fell across the sand in front of me. A bronzed hand closed around the book.

The lump in my throat was going to choke me. I couldn't breathe around it, and I couldn't swallow. But I couldn't stay there, staring at my knees either. Slowly, I dragged my gaze up and met his.

He had pretty eyes, I noticed inanely. Too pretty for that rugged face of his. The dark brown was velvety, almost soft, and spiky, curly lashes framed that velvety brown. Right now, he was watching me with an assessing stare. His gaze roamed over me before shifting to my cheek. Bluntly, he said, "That's going to bruise if you don't ice it."

I don't know why I blurted it out, but the words came rushing up my throat and I couldn't stop them.

"It's not the first time I've been bruised." Absently, I reached up and touched the mark on my face, felt the tenderness of it under my questing fingers. Nothing was broken. Sadly, I knew how that felt, too.

His mouth went tight around the corners and his eyes flattened. He carried a lot of emotion in his eyes. I couldn't really decipher what those emotions were, but they were there. One straight, thick black brow arched. "Yeah? You do anything about it?"

"Not much." I clambered to my feet and shook the sand out of my skirt before I turned back to get the rest of my stuff off the table. "I got away from him. That's about it."

"That's more than most do."

I didn't look at him as I headed off. I didn't run. But it sure as hell felt like it.

CHAPTER TWO

O ne of my sketchbooks was missing.

I hadn't noticed it until now and that meant it could have been missing for hours. Arms folded over my middle, I tried not to rock myself as I stared at the neat stack of sketchbooks.

There should be three.

The big one that I used at the beach—the one with all the images of naked people—mostly men, most of them of Lobo. A smaller one that I used if I had the urge to draw a sunset or maybe the beach after a storm. And an even smaller one that I kept to use if I had a panic attack. I'd draw ugly sketches then, usually of my ex-husband, the way he'd look as he hurt me. Then I'd burn the images, or tear them into shreds. An oddly cathartic form of art.

There should be three.

There were only two.

And the one that was missing... Oh, shit.

It was the worst one to have lost.

After getting back from the beach, I'd gone straight to the shower, locked myself inside and had a mini-breakdown. Then I'd gotten ready for the day and spent my entire time working. Several rush jobs had kept me busy, which was good because I didn't have much time to think and it was better if I didn't have to think.

But now it was late and once I'd started to go through my regular routine—had I checked the locks? I couldn't remember. I checked them once, and then went back and checked them a second, and third time. Then I couldn't remember if I'd put everything in its spot because things *looked* off.

That was because things *where* off—the missing sketchbook.

Maybe he'd gotten in—

"No," I whispered to myself, shaking my head almost violently. That wasn't it. He hadn't gotten in and none of his hired thugs had, either.

I checked everything over just in case and then I checked the security cameras.

Nobody had been inside, all day. Except me. I spent thirty minutes going over the feed and then I went over it again, focusing on just the windows and the doors.

I stood in my apartment, going through the compulsive little routines that let me think I had some modicum of privacy. Drawing all the curtains. Powering down all the electronics, especially the five cell phones. Yes, there were five because right before our second anniversary, he'd taken my phone and now I worried he'd break in and do it again, cutting me off from the outside world. If I couldn't call for help—

"You can. Stop it," I said, shoving a hand into my hair and fisting it. The phones weren't the problem. My missing sketchbook was.

A sob ripped out of me and I pressed my fingertips to my lips.

Those sketches were the one thing that was mine. Losing even one of them was like losing a piece of my soul.

Closing my eyes, I made myself think about where I'd seen it last.

I'd come home from the beach and I'd been so upset, so flustered from seeing Lo— No. His name was Jinx. I'd met him. Seeing him had flustered me and just that was enough to make me need a drink. I'd almost taken a glass of wine into the shower with me, but I'd made myself settle for a pot of tea once I dried off.

If I drank in the middle of the day, I ended up sleeping, and then I couldn't sleep at night. But I had met him.

I hadn't checked my sketchbooks. I must have left it…at the beach.

What if he saw it?

Oh, no. Horror and shame flooded me. He'd think me pathetic for sure. If he'd seen it. Those desperate, pathetic little renderings. And what if he felt offended? That was even worse. What was I thinking—

Stop it. It's art. You never meant for anybody to see it, I chided myself, trying to get a grip before the shame spiraled out of control. No, I'd never meant for anybody to see it, but I still felt naked, thinking about it out there. Naked, and exposed. More exposed than I'd felt in a long time.

Years, in fact. It wasn't quite as bad as it had been during the exams at the hospital, but it was far worse than you would think, considering all I'd done was lose a sketchbook.

Silly as it was, knowing I'd left it where others could see it, I felt violated. It was wrong of me to feel like that. I'd *been* violated. Exposed. Stripped bare. There was no reason to feel like that over a sketchbook.

Even if it did have every private and personal thing in it, thinking of it as a violation… But it was more than a sketchbook. It was my freedom. Where I could slip away from myself.

Now my escape was gone.

Moving to the window, I pushed the concealing curtains back and stared outside. And even as I did it, I saw a flash of movement from the apartment just across the street, two doors down. My despised shadow, watching me, even now.

Just then, I didn't care.

I'd left that piece of me out there.

I wouldn't sleep.

Not tonight.

I wanted to go out there and look for it.

But I couldn't.

It was already dark. And as much as I needed my sketchbook, I couldn't brave the dark.

▲▼▲

When you live in dread, time trickles by so slowly. That was the next twelve hours. Slow second by slow second, miserable hour by miserable hour.

I worked through the night. I paced. I checked the curtains, twisted the locks, went through each routine where I had to check the windows. Once, twice, three times…and it still wasn't enough. I didn't feel safe. I felt naked and there were times when I felt so dirty and filthy and the three showers I took that night weren't enough to make me feel clean.

There are numerous names for what's wrong with me.

I have post-traumatic stress syndrome, but considering everything that had been done, that was to be expected.

I had developed OCD. It didn't happen overnight. It became more apparent in the days after I came home from the hospital, staying first in a shelter for battered women, and then in an apartment one of the counselors had helped me find. The therapist I'd started seeing asked about weird habits—did I check locks, ever find myself getting up out of bed to do that?

It didn't occur to me that it was weird until she pointed out that it was interfering with my sleep, and then my daily routine. Absolutely, that counts as weird.

She explained it was a coping mechanism, a way to make myself feel safer, but we had to keep it under control. The anxiety was sort of expected, as was the post traumatic stress disorder.

I have a more simple term for it all—I'm just messed up.

My ex saw to that. Just as he promised he would.

But those sketchbooks are my way of fixing myself.

I had to get it back. Nibbling on a piece of toast, I hovered near the window and watched, waiting for the sun to rise.

Outside, it was still dark.

And that piece of me…was it still there?

I was already dressed and ready to go when the sun finally made its appearance. My stalker was on his porch, as if he'd sensed a weakness, a break in my routine.

I had my bag packed with my sketchbooks, including a new one…just in case. I expected I would need it.

It was everything else that took time. Checking the locks. The front door was locked. The back door, I'd lock on the way out.

But I had to check the windows. All tight. Nobody had touched them since last night, but I went over them just in case. All the latches were sealed. Sometimes I thought about painting them shut. But that would make them ugly and I liked to think about what it would be like if I ever felt brave enough to open them.

I checked the windows again. Then I moved to the back door, the bag hooked over my shoulder, the strap lying between my breasts. The mace was hanging from a quick-release carabiner and I could get to it in a second. All the locks, top to bottom… "Let's go," I muttered. Top one, okay. Middle, okay. Bottom two? Check. I checked them again. One more time. My hand slipped on the doorknob and I lost my place, had to start all over again.

Swallowing the knot in my throat, I clattered down the stairs, the wooden soles of my sandals clanking too loudly.

He was following me.

I don't know how he'd known I'd slid out the back door, but he was following me.

I walked faster.

I had to look for my journal.

I didn't matter that I knew I wouldn't find it.

The beach was a clean one. People came in and cleaned it every evening and there was never any trash when I visited in the morning. It didn't matter that I knew my sketchbook wasn't trash. I'd left it behind and they'd take it and throw it away.

I knew that…logically. But logic didn't matter. Its soft, gentle voice didn't have a chance to even whisper to me as I rushed across the stand.

"It's been a whole day," I told myself. "It's been one whole day. I won't find it."

I made myself say it as I rounded the bend that led to my spot. I said it out loud because I needed to prepare myself.

Swallowing the knot, I braced myself to look at my bench. Knowing it wasn't going to be there helped a little. But I had to get ready. My gaze skittered past Lobo. He was out here even this early?

Wow.

Hardly anybody was here this early.

Just a few people walking their dogs, me, my stalker…and Lobo.

Maybe he lived in one of the little homes that littered the beach like a bunch of colorful children's toys or maybe he just loved the beach as much I did. Sometimes he was in the water, swimming. A few times I'd seen him with one of the boards—not quite long enough to be a surfboard, but I didn't know what they were called.

Right now, he sat there, staring out over the water. As though he'd felt my gaze, he turned his head, and over the distance, I felt our gazes connect. The impact of that gaze rocked through me, heating my blood as it raced through my veins. Shock cut into me as I felt my body respond, all from a simple look. My nipples went tight, stabbing into the sturdy cotton of my bra and between my legs I was wet and achy. Mortified, I jerked my gaze away and focused on the picnic table where I usually sat.

For one minute, I didn't even process what I was staring at.

Then I reached up and rubbed my eyes.

Lowering my hand, I looked again.

My sketchbook was still there. Sitting on my table.

It wasn't really mine.

How could I call that rickety old picnic table mine when it was on a public beach? But it was where I always sat, where I'd sat for months. Slowly, I started across the sand, staring in rapt fascination. Had it sat there, undisturbed since yesterday?

It had rained last night. The sketches inside would be ruined.

I touched the cover.

My throat went tight as I eased the sturdy cover up and started to flip through the images. One by one. They were all fine. Nothing disturbed. I came to the last one, still waiting for me to finish it.

The one of Lobo's hands. I traced the line of his palm, stroking my finger along the sketched line.

I had my sketchbook.

I could go back now.

My heart seized inside my chest when I caught sight of the man who lived across the street. He was standing there.

Staring at me.

An insolent smile curled his lips.

Slowly, I turned around and sat down at the table. My hands shook as I pressed them flat to the old, scarred wooden surface. Closing my eyes, I whispered, "You're you. You're free. You escaped."

Smoothing the long, loose folds of my wrap skirt around me, I reached inside my bag and dug out one of my pencils.

I wasn't going back inside my damn house.

Not yet.

The sketch of his hands took up most of that morning.

At some point, the man who did nothing but watch me left.

At some point, more people arrived at the beach.

It was going to be a hot day. I could already feel the sweat gathering at the nape of my neck. Several hours had passed since I'd sat down at the table and my back ached, my hands cramped.

But I was smiling.

My sketchbook had been here.

And I hadn't let that bastard chase me back into the house. Slowly, I arched my back and twisted, working some of the kinks out before reaching for one of the rags I kept with me so I could clean the charcoal from my hands.

A breeze kicked up and blew my hair into my face. I squinted and put the rag down before finding a clip in my bag. As I was twisting my hair back, I looked up and saw Lobo.

He was sitting one table away.

One.

When he sat—*if* he sat—it was usually in the sand down closer to the water.

His eyes rested on me. He sat with studied casualness on the picnic table—the top of it, not the seat—hands braced behind him, and next to him were two bottles of water.

I recognized the label. Aquafina.

And I also couldn't help but notice that he stared at me.

That damn knot that always settled in my throat decided to make another appearance. Slowly, I looked away and focused on gathering up my supplies. I'd had over three hours. I didn't need to start anything else. Soon, I'd need to get to work on the projects I had up for the day.

There was that one cover… I was going to have fun with it. It was a male/male project and the—

My jaw dropped open.

The wind had blown the pages of my sketchbook.

And on the back of the sketch I'd just finished were the words:

If you're going to spend that much time drawing me, maybe you'd like to get my name.

I'd definitely like yours.

He'd seen.

Oh, fuck. He had seen it. That intimate picture, that dream I'd dared to let myself have while I was awake, of me on my knees in front of him. A dream that even now filled me with longing. He had seen.

He had looked through my sketches, just as I'd feared.

I'd definitely like yours.

I moved off that seat quicker than I could remember moving in my entire life.

I still wasn't fast enough.

Before I'd even managed to shove all my supplies into the appliquéd bag I'd bought at a street fair last year, he was there.

The bottle of water was put in front of me.

The table groaned under his weight as he sat down.

My throat was dry and I hated how much I really wanted to grab that bottle of water.

"My name is Dillian."

His name. He'd given me his name.

That meant—

I swallowed. What did it mean?

Nothing. It meant nothing. I needed to get out of there. But instead of getting out of there, I shot him a look, swallowing around the damn lump.

My voice came out huskier than normal. "That kid the other day called you Jinx."

From the corner of my eye, I saw him smile. "My last name is Jenkins. Some of the guys around here call me Jenks. Nickname. Dillian Jenkins. Jenks." Then his lashes drooped over his eyes and that smile changed. "Or, if you want, Lobo. I don't really mind. What's your name?"

I slid the strap of my bag into place, settled it so that it ran between my breasts.

A quiet sigh drifted to me as I turned away.

Abruptly, I stopped. I hated this. Hated being so afraid. He'd seen those intimate images I'd put to paper and it hadn't bothered him. Or maybe it had and he'd decided not to let it. I didn't know. But he was over here talking to me and that had to count for something. I couldn't keep running away. I was so fucking tired of it. Reaching into the bag, I ripped out the sketch of his hands. I couldn't quite manage to talk normally just yet, but I could do that. Scrawling my name in the bottom right corner, I told myself it counted. Signing it was almost the same thing, right?

He was rising to his feet when I turned and put it down, using the water bottle to keep it from blowing away.

I didn't wait to see if he took it.

▲▼▲

I didn't go back on Friday.

I couldn't stay in my house, but I wasn't ready to look at Jenks either. Dillian didn't seem to suit him and I couldn't call him Lobo now that I knew his name. But Jenks worked. Jinx worked better in my mind, but I wouldn't strip a person of his name.

I knew what it was like to be stripped of something as basic and vital as your identity. I wouldn't do it to anybody else.

Since I had to go somewhere, I went to a new art supply store I'd seen mentioned online. It was on the other side of town and my stalker couldn't follow me.

As much as he knew my routine, I knew his.

He had weekly appointments on Fridays.

I suspected he had to check with a parole officer. I didn't consider myself as being judgmental. Seth was the one who helped me figure it out and he'd volunteered to help make the guy leave me alone.

But I'd said if it wasn't that man, it would be somebody else.

At least I knew this devil.

So he'd watched along with me and told me the man was an ex-con. "Once you've done time, you get to know the type. He's the type. He's probably meeting a parole officer on Fridays. I don't like this, Shadow. I don't like it at all," he'd said.

Neither did I.

But it was routine and I'd take routine over something unknown any day.

The art store was a bit of a flop. The selection was limited and more focused on pottery and jewelry making, but there was a bookstore next to it. I found myself staring at the books displayed in the window and yearning.

It had been a long time since I'd let myself read.

I could even remember just when I'd stopped.

Age twenty-two. I'd finished cleaning the house and it had been three-thirty. He wouldn't have been home for another two hours and I should have had almost thirty minutes to read before I had to start getting ready. There was so much I had to do before he came home.

But he came home early that day and he found me climbing up off the couch with a book clutched in my hands.

I hadn't been properly ready to greet him.

My fingers trembled as I reached up to touch my cheek.

Yes, I knew how broken bones felt. In the arm. The ribs. The face.

I stared at the books in the window, all but shaking with fear. Then I walked into the store. He stopped controlling me when I made that happen.

That time was now. I used to love to read. I'd find that in me again.

▲▼▲

It was past midnight before I was able to settle all the books in their places. Getting back inside the house had taken too long and I'd been late. Twenty books didn't seem like a lot, not when I hadn't bought them in so long. But it was a lot and I couldn't sleep until they were all in their place.

I hadn't been able to do it earlier though because I had to work.

I had to start work at one and I couldn't deviate from that.

So the books would wait until later and later meant after seven because that was time to eat. Then it was time to get ready for bed but I couldn't get ready for bed until the doors were checked and the windows.

Then the books.

I found spots for each one. They couldn't just go on a bookshelf. I had them, but most of the shelves were used for other things. In that hell where I had lived with my ex, we'd used bookshelves for books—boring things, the classics and books on philosophy and finance and history. All educational things that would broaden my world view. The books he'd wanted me to read. The books I hated.

I'd bought books just like them when I moved here. And I used them... to make bookshelves. All it took was scissors, glue, L-brackets and screws. Those precious, hated books that he'd insisted I learned to enjoy, well, I'd finally done it. I enjoyed seeing how they held up the things I enjoyed. Cookbooks and texts on art.

Now the "invisible" shelves also held a few of the romances, including a copy of the Nora Roberts book I'd been reading when he came in that day and broke my right cheekbone. He told the doctors I'd tripped and smashed my face into the coffee table because I was reading and walking at the same time. I'd never finished the book.

I'd gathered up all of my books and thrown them out, as soon as I healed.

Standing in the doorway, I stared at the Nora book and told myself that I would finish it.

One day.

But not today.

I'm dreaming...

It was the only thing that made sense.

Because in my dream, Jenks was in my bedroom and he sprawled across my bed while I stood across from him with my sketchbook, drawing him.

He was naked.

My cheeks heated as my gaze ran over him, lingering on the muscles in his belly, and lower. He had a thin strip of hair that started low, curling around his navel and then thickening around his cock. And his cock was thick, heavy, growing long and hard as I stared at him.

Blood rushed to my cheeks as he reached down and closed a hand around his length, stroked himself from his balls up to the very tip, the plum-shaped end disappearing behind his fist before emerging as he started the downward stroke.

"You're a rude little girl," he murmured.

I jerked my eyes upward. "Wuh-what?"

A wicked smile curved his lips. "You're rude. Staring at me like that."

"It's my dream, I can stare if I want to."

"And what about when it's not a dream?"

"That won't happen." I shook my head and focused on my sketch. I don't know why I bothered. It wouldn't be there when I woke up. But maybe the memory would be. I placed each line carefully and shot another look at him.

My breath hitched as I saw him standing right in front of me, just a few scant inches away.

"What...what are you doing here?"

He reached up and cupped my cheek. "Since it's your dream, I figured I'd make it worthwhile. You can do more in your dream than look, Shadow. You can touch."

And then his mouth took mine.

▲▼▲

I woke with the dream taste of him on my mouth.

In my mind, he tasted of the ocean, maybe beer and man.

And the bitch of it all was, now I craved the taste of him for real. That kiss made me remember how long it had been since I'd felt wanted. Needed.

Back in high school, I'd had a couple of boyfriends and I'd dated. I had liked dating. My parents had been fairly strict, but once I'd been forced to go live with my aunt, she hadn't cared. She actually preferred it if I wasn't home, and so had I. So I'd dated a *lot*.

Then there had been that one year between high school and college, and...yes, there had been more than a few boys, some even closer to men. There had been guys I'd dated in college, too. Some I'd really *liked*. Then I'd met my ex-husband. He'd been older, so funny and charming and sweet, and he seemed...so perfect. He bought me gifts, went out of his way to learn the things I liked, showed up at the art shop where I worked— things that had seemed terribly romantic at the time.

I'd let him sweep me off my feet, and then he'd devastated my life, and had come very close to ending it.

A year ago, two years...the thought of letting a man touch me would have horrified me.

But now I wanted it.

I missed it.

It had been ages since I'd kissed a man. Since a man had kissed me.

Since a man had wanted me.

I'd forgotten what it was like to be wanted. My ex had wanted to *control* me, to *own* me, but he'd never *wanted* me. That damn dream had made me remember everything I was missing.

I almost hated Jenks in that moment.

Moving to the window, I stared outside, watching as the sun danced off the water.

He'd be there.

I shouldn't go back.

But I knew I would.

CHAPTER THREE

This time, he didn't bring me a bottle of water.

He sat down across from me barely fifteen minutes after I'd started to sketch and he plunked a bowl of ice cream down two inches from my hand.

I curled my fingers into my palm to keep from reaching for the spoon.

It was mango, from the Roadside. I knew, because every once in a while I let myself indulge and I loved their mango ice cream.

For a long, heart-racing moment, I stared at the ice cream, ever aware of the mace hanging from the clip on my bag. It was a few scant inches away. Could I get to it in time and could I incapacitate him? He was so big. And he looked as if he knew how to move.

On Saturdays, twice a month, I still went to self-defense classes. My instructors had taken to pairing me with large men lately, but he was so very large and his presence, for lack of a better word, was just so *there*.

How did he know I liked mango ice cream?

How did he know I liked *ice cream*, period?

Was he watching me?

Was I paranoid?

Fear slammed away inside me and I fought the urge to run, the urge to scream.

Finally, I laid down the pencil I'd been using and instead of staring at the ice cream, I lifted my face to his and asked bluntly, "What is that?"

"It's ice cream," he said, and in the back of his eyes, I thought I saw a smile, but it was there and gone again, gone so fast I almost missed it.

"Why?"

"It's ice cream because they made it that way," he said, his voice reasonable.

"Are you often this obtuse with women?"

"Are you often this difficult when somebody buys you ice cream?"

I pushed the bowl away. "Why did you buy me ice cream?"

"Because I thought you might like it." Then he glanced down at the sketchbook and added, "And because I want to see more of what you're working on...and maybe get your name."

"I told you my name."

I eyed the ice cream, acutely aware of the hunger gnawing at my belly. I hadn't eaten since dinner yesterday and I'd only picked at it then. Until now, I hadn't wanted anything, but I wanted that ice cream.

"You did?"

I shot him a look. "It was on the picture I gave you."

He pushed the ice cream toward me. "It's yours," he said, his voice level, neutral. "If you want it, eat it. Otherwise it's going to melt."

I took it.

After I'd eaten three bites, he said, "Shadow. That was written in the corner. That's really your name?"

Slowly, I nodded. "That's what my birth certificate says."

The ice cream was so good—sweet and rich. I'd just have a few bites.

Five minutes later, the bowl was empty. Blinking in surprise, I put the spoon inside it and set it down.

"You look like you need more."

"No." I squirmed on the seat and bent back over the sketchbook. "Thank you. That was nice of you." *Please go away now.*

"You going to let me see any more of your work?"

"This isn't work." I gripped the pencil.

"Then what is it?"

Escape.

I heard paper crumpling.

Something unfolded and then he pushed it into my line of site. It was...well, art. Sorta. Erotic art. Like nothing I'd ever seen.

If the nudes I did made me squirm even as I drew, then this made me clench my thighs together and my breathing came faster just starting at it.

And the face...

It was CGI-rendered, I could tell that much despite the wrinkles and creases in the paper. And despite the wrinkles and creases in the paper, one thing that was very clear, the face looked a lot like mine.

Jerking my head up, I stared at him. "What the hell is that?" I demanded, my voice stark.

"Well, it looks a lot like you," he mused, propping his elbows on the table. He reached out a hand and dragged the image closer, tracing one finger down the mermaid's tail before going back up the other side and outlining her breast.

And my nipples tightened in response, as though he'd been toying with mine, not touching a stupid piece of paper.

Swallowing, I found that I couldn't look away this time when he shifted his attention up and stared at me.

"I showed you mine." Dark brown eyes bored into mine. "You going to show me yours?"

"You did this?" I couldn't decide if I was horrified or amazed. The whimsical, sexy little mermaid, one hand lifted to toy with her own nipple, her face tipped to catch the sun, and the expression of longing—that was something I'd never been. She wore what she felt on her face, and I locked everything inside. She had her free hand outstretched as though she wasn't too afraid to reach for it.

And here I was with a man I did want, right there. All he wanted to do was talk to me and I was terrified, nausea churning and twisting in my belly.

"Nah. I don't have that kind of talent. But I excel at noticing things. And I couldn't help but notice that she looks like you." He reached over and touched the edge of her tail. Part of me almost thought I could feel the ghostly echo of his hand on my thigh. "So…you going to let me see anything else?"

I was tempted.

But trust didn't come so easily.

Slowly, I shook my head. "Not today. Maybe next week."

His lids drooped low. "How about a deal…what about Friday night? I could pick you up for dinner, you could bring the sketches then."

"No." It barely came out as a whisper. A date…he'd just asked me out on a date. Even as some part of me was almost excited at the idea of it, the rest of me shut down. I couldn't date.

Not him.

Not anybody.

Not ever.

Jenks didn't give up.

Three weeks after the first time he'd asked me out, I arrived at the beach to find a red cloth spread across my table. There was a picnic basket. Two plates. Something twisted in my gut—disappointment, I knew that feeling well. Even as I went to turn away and find a different table, he came walking up and he wasn't wearing what he always wore. His standard clothing consisted of two options: board shorts with a tank top or board shorts without a tank top.

So I almost didn't recognize him when I saw him wearing a pair of dark khaki trousers, rolled up over his ankles to stay out of the sand and a white polo shirt.

I pinched the bridge of my nose, then lowered my hand as he came to a stop in front of me. "You ready to eat lunch?"

"I…ah…" I looked at him, then back at the table.

"We're having a picnic," he told me.

"We are?" Deep inside, I felt the first rumblings of irritation. I didn't want to be told what or how I'd spend my time. Not anymore. Even something as innocuous as a picnic. Even if it was a sunny day and I hadn't eaten. I'd been controlled before by a man who told me when I'd eat and what I'd eat and how I'd eat. I'd never go back there again.

A look that might have been caution flickered in his eyes and I looked over at him. "Ah…well, maybe I should I rephrase that." He ran his tongue across his lips as he rocked back on his heels, head cocked as he studied me. "I am having a picnic. I planned on eating here since I already put my blanket down. You can join me if you want to. But I'm going to."

Some of the frustration I felt started to ease as he settled down at the table. For a moment, I watched him, watched the shirt stretch across his biceps as he dug into the picnic hamper and pulled out potato salad, sliced deli meat, avocado.

I shot a look up on the beach, saw some of Dillian's friends. A few women had glanced toward us as they moved by. He could have talked to any of them. He wanted to be here with me. Maybe he was just hung up on looking at the sketches, although he hadn't asked about them for the past week or so.

My feet felt heavy as I moved to join him.

A bit of a smile curved his lips as I settled down across from him. "Thank you," he murmured.

"I don't like being told what I'm going to do."

"I'll keep that in mind," he said softly. He put everything between us and dug out serving spoons and a knife for the condiments. "How much of it has to do with your ex?"

I froze and shot him a look.

"You've already told me you know what it's like to be bruised." Then he nodded at my hand. "You can still see where you wore the wedding ring."

Slowly, I looked down, barely able to make out the faint white strip on my left ring finger. I'd taken the ring off months ago. But there were days when I'd compulsively put it back on, days when it seemed as though my ex was closer than normal, breathing down my neck, and just waiting to make an appearance.

It's a terrible thing to live with that kind of fear, even when you can feel yourself trying to move away from it. Maybe then it's even worse— you can almost taste the freedom, but the fear holds you hostage.

Curling my hand into a fist, I stared at the slightly paler strip of flesh on my hand where the ring had been, then I looked up and met his eyes. "I don't want to talk about this."

"Then don't." A humorless smile curved his lips, but it did nothing to lighten his features. If anything, it gave him a slightly devilish look. "I figure you answered the question just fine. I just hope the bastard is off rotting in a ditch somewhere."

I thought of my ex, sitting in his posh gallery, smoking one of his thin cigars as he dictated to one of the secretaries he'd liked to fuck while he'd been married to me. One of them had become his mistress. Then he'd discarded her, moved on to another one. It had been his cycle and I had no doubt he'd continued it. He'd moved on to a bigger gallery and even expanded, opening one in Chicago, then in Seattle.

His life was going so very well.

And mine was still in shambles.

"No," I said, reaching for the bottle of water he'd put out before I'd even arrived. "He's not."

"Do you want him to be?"

To my surprise, it startled a laugh out of me.

The rest of the picnic passed in an almost comfortable silence and when I was ready to go, I did something that surprised me. Even though I'd been carrying it around for just that purpose, I hadn't known if I'd be able to do it.

But I did it.

I'd brought one of my older sketchbooks with me—had been carrying it for a week now, although I'd lacked the courage to show him. Now, holding my breath, I pulled it out of my bag and left it sitting on the table.

CHAPTER FOUR

It was a date that really wasn't.

That was what I told myself. After all, we ran into each other on the street.

A couple times a month, Marla, Seth and I had pizza night.

They'd started it not long after Marla realized I really didn't *do* anything. She'd wanted to change that. At first, she'd tried inviting me out to go shopping or hit a bar with her and Seth, but I wasn't up for either of those. At least not at the time.

So we'd started doing a movie night, then pizza night.

It had taken her a month to talk me into it the first time, but movie night, then pizza night slowly became a regular thing.

Tonight should have been pizza night.

But this was their anniversary. They'd been together for two years, living together for one year and although Marla didn't know it, Seth was going to propose. He loved her, he'd told me, for real loved her and he wanted to marry her.

And they were off to Savannah for a long weekend. They'd come back with her starry-eyed, him grinning like a fool. Maybe I could help with the wedding. That might be fun.

But it meant when Sunday rolled around, it was pizza night and I couldn't stay stuck in the house.

I had to stick to my schedule.

It didn't *matter* that they weren't here.

I knew it was pizza night so I had to go get pizza.

I hated that eight o'clock came and went and I was nervous and shaking, all because I couldn't think beyond the fact that it was past eight and I was still in the house.

It took forty minutes because I had to check and recheck the locks, the windows, the doors, the locks and then the doors one last time. It's harder when you're nervous, because when you're nervous, you mess up the routine, but I had to check. Finally, at almost ten 'til nine, I escaped the house. The balmy air of a Carolina evening wrapped around me but I was too frazzled, too frustrated and too upset to notice. One foot after the other, I walked to our pizza place. I'd have to eat alone. I hated eating alone.

People stared.

They watched you.

What if somebody recognized me—

A hand touched my arm.

I reacted out of instinct, driving a stiffened hand into a vulnerable neck, bringing up my knee to strike the groin. My hand connected. My knee bounced off a rock-hard thigh and then I was caught, pinned up against the nearest window while I panicked and bucked and twisted to get away.

"Shadow…calm down. Shadow!"

Another hand caught my wrists. Dazed, I found myself staring into Jenks' eyes.

His hand cupped my face and he peered down at me.

He held my hands in one fist, not tightly, just enough to keep me from pulling away.

"You with me?"

I sucked in a desperate breath.

"That's it. Take another one," he murmured. "I think I'll do the same."

He grimaced and I saw that his face was a strange shade of red.

He blew out his breath and then slowly uncurled his hand from my wrists. "You've got some moves," he murmured. "I scared you. I'm sorry."

The only thing I wanted to do was curl in on myself and just die.

As though he sensed my intentions, he kept his body between me and the escape route back to my house. His other hand stayed on my shoulder while he talked. "I saw you walking," he said, forcing a smile. I could see the strain around the edges and part of me was glad he felt as weird about this as I did. "I wanted to say hi."

He paused, grimaced. "Hi."

The absurdity of it almost made me laugh. Instead I just stared at him for a minute and then murmured, "Hi."

"What are you doing on this fine night? Other than beating up guys who mistakenly touch you?"

Blood rushed to my cheeks and I tried to pull back. The glass behind me prevented that.

Jenks swore. "Son of a bitch... I didn't mean it like that, baby. I just... hell. I should have known better. I was an idiot. I'm sorry, okay?"

His eyes stayed on my face. How did I answer that? I didn't know.

He eased back. "Look, I just... Don't take off, okay? I never see you away from the beach and as soon as twelve thirty rolls around, you take off. I just wanted to see if we could get something to eat. That maybe-next-week date you keep teasing me about."

No hovered on the tip of my tongue.

I don't know what possessed me to say yes.

Whatever it was, that yes landed me at the pizza place with Dillian Jenkins.

And three hours passed before I knew it.

Standing outside of the pizza place, I twisted the short strap of my clutch around my fingers and looked up at Jenks, tried to figure out the right way to say goodbye before he could offer to walk me home.

I didn't want him doing that. I didn't want him watching me as I searched the porch and the yard, searched for some sign that my sanctuary had been invaded. I didn't want him to realize that the man in the corner was watching us and that he'd follow us home.

His hand brushed my cheek and I looked up at him, my heart leaping up to hammer in my throat.

Soft, dark eyes watched me and he lowered his head. I froze, too terrified to bolt as I should, my knees locked, my belly twisting in mad circles.

He didn't kiss me, though.

Instead, he pressed his mouth to my ear and spoke.

The words didn't make sense at first.

Then, as they started to connect, a bizarre sense of helplessness, frustration and denial spun inside me, an emotional hurricane that bounced around, seeking a weak spot to break free and wreak havoc.

"There's a guy who's been watching you since you came in here."

As he straightened back up, he canted his chin off to the side.

I didn't have to look for him.

I knew he was there.

He made no attempt to hide himself, leaning against the bar, digging through a bowl of nuts and crunching on them.

Curling my hands into fists, I turned away and headed for the door.

As I did, two men started to shadow me.

One was the man hired by my ex.

The other was Jenks.

As I shoved through the doors, desperate for air, Jenks had his hand at my back and once I broke free of the crush of people, I was pathetically grateful for that supporting touch. "You look like you want to puke," he said shifting his hand from my back to my arm and attempting to guide me over to the wall.

My stalker had headed down the walk, loitering in the area as if he was looking for a place to smoke. He didn't leave. He just chose a different piece of the pavement to pollute.

I resisted Jenks' attempts to get me out of the middle of the sidewalk. I didn't know what to do, though. To get to my house, I had to go the other direction, pass the bastard who had been watching me. Who was *still* watching. I couldn't stay out here all night.

Without understanding what drove me, I pushed away from him and moved to the crosswalk. The ebb and flow of people around me usually drove me crazy, but just then, it felt…comforting. I didn't feel as exposed as I usually did and I knew that the man watching me couldn't see me as clearly. He was on his feet now and trying to weave through the people. Jenks didn't have that problem. He was so big, he just plowed right through them. Either they yielded or he just pushed them aside.

"You don't look surprised that you've got a guy following you." He had his hands in his pockets as we moved onto the sidewalk a minute later and separated from the crowd.

The light had changed halfway through and the punk was still trying to catch up. I put some speed on, the little purse I held swinging from my hand, my breath coming in faster, choppier gasps as we rounded the corner onto the street that would lead to the beach.

"Here."

Jenks caught my elbow and tugged me into an alcove.

The little coffee shop that served coffee everything—coffee ice cream, coffee candy, and just plain coffee. It was closed now and I turned to look at him, but he had his hand on my shoulder and was looking out into the street. The second I moved to brush past him, I saw the man again.

The one from the bar.

Jenks shot out a hand, fisted it into the man's T-shirt, and then jerked him into the alcove. My breath caught and hitched as he slammed his prey up against the glass door. "Well, well, well…" He cocked his head and studied the man closely. "I caught myself a rat."

Swallowing the taste of fear crowding my throat, I tucked into the shadows and wrapped my arms around myself. While Jenks glowered down at the man he outweighed and outreached, I eyed the space between them and the wall. I could squeeze through there. And now, I wasn't being watched. I could get back to my place, lock myself inside—

"Why you following her?"

"I don't know what the fuck you're talking about."

Jenks slammed him up against the brick wall, hard enough that the guy's teeth might have rattled around in his head. Oddly fascinated, I watched. Then, as I continued to gape, Jenks shoved his hand in the guy's front pocket. Scowling, he did the same to the other one. This time, he came up with a wallet. "Let's just see who we're dealing with." Without letting go of the guy's shirtfront, he one-handedly flipped the wallet open. "Les Borbeck. Nice picture, Les. You lie like a dog on your license. If you're six-one and one-eighty, then I'm Papa Smurf."

He smacked the wallet up against Borbeck's chest and Borbeck scrambled to catch it, and then he must have just been scrambling to breathe because in the time it took me to process what was happening, Jenks went from holding him by the front of his shirt to jamming his forearm under Borbeck's jaw. He pushed in and up, pressing so hard that Borbeck's face went red and he rose up on his toes just to alleviate the pressure.

"Now." Jenks' tone didn't change. "You're going to answer me this time or I'll rip it out of you. Why are you following her? And don't give me that shit that you're not. I saw you down the street, on the opposite side when I started talking to her. You walked right past us, and then you show up in the same restaurant. You leave at the same time. You're following her. Now tell me why?"

Two seconds of silence passed and I felt compelled to tell him. Somebody needed to talk. I could all but taste the violence in the air.

Then, as I fought to push the words out, Borbeck lost his struggle and the answer came ripping out. "It's her husband—he's paying me. Two hundred a day. It's easy money. She never does shit and I just have to watch her. If she sees me, it's not a big deal and he just wants to know what she does and who she talks to. It's all legal as long as I don't get close." The words all but tumbled over themselves to get out of his throat and his eyes wheeled around in his head to land on my face. "Please! It ain't like I'm hurting ya!"

I flinched as the words slammed into me. He had no idea what he was doing to me.

Rubbing my fingers over my mouth, I pushed past them both, my legs wobbling, locking my knees, trying to keep them from giving out on me.

A few minutes later, a pair of motorcycle boots appeared in my line of vision. I kept on walking. I went right past my house, seeking out the path that would lead to the beach.

I wanted my table.

The beach was all but deserted now.

It had to be close to midnight.

Sinking down on the surface of the table, I braced my elbows on my knees and stared at the night-dark water.

"Are you still married to him?" Jenks asked, his voice soft in the quiet of the night.

Looking down at my toes, I entwined my fingers and pressed my palms together. Then, closing my eyes, I lifted my hands, as though I was in prayer and pressed them to my brow. Softly, I murmured, "No. I divorced him three years ago. He still thinks I'm his, though. As long as he's alive, he'll never let me go."

Warm, strong fingers closed around my hands, guided them down. "Why weren't you surprised he had somebody following you?" Jenks asked, his voice soft, but there was a thread of steel in it.

He'd push for that answer. Even if he had to wait, and wait, he would, until he received it.

"Because he's had me watched every day since I left the shelter," I responded. "There was somebody on the plane when I flew out here. Somebody in the first neighborhood where I lived, and in this one. Sometimes, if I'm lucky, I can sneak out the back door and come out here and the guy who watches me doesn't know I've left. But most of the time, if I leave the house, I'm watched."

"Why don't you report it?"

Sighing, I pressed my fingers to my eyes. "It's not as easy as that. And I know because I tried. He's a rich son of a bitch and unless one of the men he hires would be willing to testify *against* him and risk getting their own asses in trouble? It's my word against his. His father was a lawyer—most of the family went into law. He grew up knowing the ins and outs of the law, almost went into it himself. He has done some of the most vile acts imaginable and nobody believed *anything* I said. He knows how to work people, how to twist things. Within five minutes, he'll have you convinced I'm crazy and out to hurt myself and he only has people watching me so he can be there to save me the next time I try to slit my wrists or have marathon drinking sessions with bunch of pill chasers or—"

His hands came down on the table, hard.

Startled, I jerked my gaze up and met his.

"Stop," he said. Earlier, his voice had been level and easy, no anger showing. Now he practically shook with it. "Don't say shit like that about yourself, okay?"

"What, that I'm crazy?" I leaned back, desperate to get some room between us. I could feel the heat of him on my skin and it went licking through me, a teasing, taunting torment of all the things I'd never feel again.

In the dead of night, the silvery moonlight shining down on us, I couldn't see him well. His eyes were like bottomless pools of pure velvet and I could just fall in and lose myself. Part of me wanted to do just that.

"Yes." He lifted one hand, placed it on my breastbone. The heat of it was a shock and until that moment, I hadn't realized I was cold. Now, I couldn't stop shivering.

"Why not?" I stared at him. "It's the truth. After what he did to me, it's a miracle I'm not crazier than I am."

"Stop." He shook his head.

I laughed softly. "You know, if anybody should be upset by the fact that my sanity is somewhat questionable, it's *me*. But it's nothing more than the truth. I have PTSD, I suffer from panic attacks that almost incapacitate me, and I deal with OCD now—things I never had before he got hold of me. My fear of him still runs my life, and I *know* it. If that doesn't certify me as mental, then what does it make me?"

"A survivor." The words were delivered in a flat, hard voice. "I don't need to know what he did to you, unless you're ready to tell me. But I know a survivor when I see one."

I stilled, caught off guard.

His eyes held me captive as he leaned in, his breath a soft, warm caress on my cheek. "A survivor…damaged, determined. And so damn brave. The last woman on earth I should want. But fuck it all. I still want you."

I blinked, my lashes drooping low as I watched him through them. That concealing veil wasn't enough to hide behind, though. His hand slid higher, curved around my neck and tangled in my hair, tugging my head back.

He stared down at me. "Tell me to stop."

CHAPTER FIVE

Simple words.

Easy words.

And if I thought about it for even a minute, maybe that's just what I'd do. Tell him to stop.

Instead, I dropped my gaze and stared at his mouth.

I knew that mouth, almost intimately.

I say *almost*, because you can't really know a person's body intimately until you've touched that body, studied it, learned it with your hands... maybe even with your mouth. Tasted it with your own, felt it against your own.

A harsh groan ripped out of him and then his mouth covered mine and the world faded away.

For a few brief moments, nothing else existed. Not even fear.

It was just him and me, and that incredible kiss.

His taste—it was every bit as addictive as I'd dreamed. And more.

He tasted like pizza and beer, like summer and sunshine and man. He tasted like an obsession that I could never let myself have and I wanted to gorge on him and never let go.

Reaching for him, I curled my hands into the front of his shirt and opened for him as his tongue sought entrance. This was no gentle, seeking kiss. This wasn't a man who was asking permission or even courting me. He wanted...and he took. He wanted...and I wanted to *give* him everything he wanted.

His arm hooked around the back of my neck while his free hand skimmed down my back and then gripped my hip, tugging me up against him. Nerves warred inside me and I tensed.

His mouth left mine and moved to my ear. "You're here, with me. Remember that. And I'm not going to hurt you."

I sucked in a breath as I fell back away from him, catching my weight on my hands as he reached for the string tie on the front of the poet-style blouse I wore. I watched his hands. He watched me. And as the lapels of the shirt fell open, blood rushed up to stain my cheeks red but it never occurred to me to make him stop.

The back of his fingers scraped roughly against my skin and sensory memory slashed at me. Times when I'd gone with *nothing*—

His hand tangled in my hair again.

"You're with *me*."

His teeth nipped my lip and I sucked in a breath, held it until my head spun. And then I blinked and focused on his face as he spread open the neckline of my shirt. Slowly, he straightened, staring down at me. Cool air danced along my flesh and I shivered, even though I wasn't really cold. I just needed—

His hands cupped my breasts.

That.

I needed that.

Hands on me, flesh against my flesh.

Squeezing my eyes shut, I bit down on my lip to keep from whimpering.

"Why don't you look at me?"

Slowly, I forced my lids open and stared up at Jenks' shadowed face. As our gazes locked, he laid one hand on my knee and stroked upward. "You hide in these clothes. Who the fuck would have guessed you look like some kind of forties movie star under all these clothes?"

The oxygen disappeared.

He laughed a little, his thumb tracing over the skin he'd bared as he pushed the skirt higher. "All soft curves and pale skin, kept hidden away." He slanted me a look and rasped, "I like it. You're like a present, wrapped up and waiting to be discovered." He pushed the skirt all the way up to my hips and then I gasped as he pulled me to the edge of the table. "I just discovered you, too. What else is there to find, Shadow?"

A whimper rose in my throat, then died as he stroked his thumb over the heat gathering between my thighs. He scraped across the bud of my clit and that light touch, just that light touch, after years of *nothing*, was more than I could handle.

Locked and rigid, blind to anything and everything, I started to shudder, then shake.

And Jenks, damn him, realized what was happening.

Nudging aside the simple, sturdy cotton of my panties, he found me underneath, naked and exposed…bare. And then he touched me again. Again, and again, until I shattered. Right there. On the picnic table where I'd first sighted him.

I climaxed, and as I started to whimper his name, he caught the sound of it against his mouth.

I was crying when it ended.

And sobbing, almost uncontrollably, before the tremors left me.

He didn't ask any questions.

If nothing else, I was grateful for that.

That was one of the two thoughts on my mind as we started up the walk back to the street.

The second thought—I needed to find another beach.

I didn't know how I'd face him after that, and I was almost positive he wasn't going to want to see me. Talk about stripping yourself bare. I'd told him how messed up I was, and then I'd showed him. He'd brought me to climax with barely a touch, and then I'd broken down into tears before I'd even had a chance to catch my breath.

Blindly, I started to walk away from him once we reached the street but I didn't make it far before his hands caught my shoulders. And then I was engulfed by him, his strong arms wrapping around me, his chin tucked against my shoulder while he murmured something nonsensical against my temple.

Holding still, barely able to breathe, I stood there.

Finally, I let myself breathe, let myself think. "What are you doing?" I asked woodenly.

"Waiting for you to stop panicking." He rubbed his cheek against my hair.

"I'm not panicking." *This* wasn't panicking. Panicking was clawing against a locked door until your fingers were bloody nubs. Panicking was screaming until your throat was raw, even though you knew nobody would hear you. This wasn't panicking. But I couldn't tell him that.

"Then I'm waiting for you to stop trying to walk away from me, stop trying to shut me out. Where are you off to in such a hurry, sugar?" he whispered as he turned his face into my hair.

"It's late. I want to go home."

"Then I'll walk you home."

I couldn't keep myself from stiffening up. "No."

"I plan on doing that whether you like it or not, Shadow," he said, and there was a thread of steel under his voice. "You've got some asshole following you and you've already told me this isn't a new thing. I'll make sure you get home safe, period."

"That's not necessary." I tugged against his arms half-heartedly, even though the feel of him, the heat—just the *touch*—was such a sweet, sweet relief that I didn't even *want* him to let me go.

He didn't, either.

"Can you tell me that you know for a fact you're safe?" he asked, his voice all too reasonable.

Safe. For some reason, just hearing that word made me laugh. It wasn't a happy sound. It was dry and broken and brittle and I laughed until I could feel myself hovering on the edge of tears again. Tearing away from him, I paced forward, putting distance between us. "*Safe?*" I spat out, glaring at him. My hair fell into my face, and angrily, I shoved it back. "Safe is an illusion. There is no such thing as *safe.*"

"So you just let some bastard control you like that? Stalk you all the time?" he asked, his voice so reasonable I wanted to hit him.

My hand curled into a fist. The urge was *that* strong. "What would *you* know about it?"

"I know that if I had some sick fuck watching me, the last thing I would do is just *ignore* it." He closed the distance between us, staring down at me. "Are you going to live this way the rest of your life? Have you called the cops? Tried to make it stop?"

"Yes!" I shouted it, the sound tearing out of me, harsh and jagged. "There was one guy, a friend of mine, who even offered to testify after my ex tried to bribe him into watching me. Seth had cops at his door two days later. He's an ex-con and his parole officer had to go to bat for him. He could have gone back to jail, *all* because he was kind to me. It's *that* easy for my ex to try to fuck up my friend's life. And a week later, he showed up and *he* was the one watching me."

"Get a damn restraining order!"

I laughed, shaking my head. "Are you *that* naïve? Really? He showed up in the coffee shop I used to like, claimed he was meeting a *friend* there, wanted to discuss investing in some real estate around here. And what do you know? The friend was *there*, claimed they'd had a meeting set up for months, decided they'd swing by that coffee shop just out of the blue, his idea, of course." Swiping a shaking hand over my mouth, I turned away. "I can't keep him out of South Carolina, Jenks! And of course since no charges were filed against him, I'd have a hard time even getting a damn restraining order."

Closing my eyes, I worried the tie on my blouse.

So few had even believed me.

A man like him wouldn't *really* keep a woman locked away in a basement room for almost a year. It couldn't happen. People would notice. They would suspect. It couldn't happen, right?

Except it had.

Tears clogged my throat and I held them at bay through sheer force of will alone. If I broke down here, I might never stop crying.

I'd humiliated myself in front of Jenks quite enough.

Woodenly, I said, "If you insist on following me home, fine. But don't tell me how to handle my ex-husband. You have no idea what he put me through, what he's still putting me through. If you haven't *been* where I have, you have no idea how you would handle a damn thing."

Then, without looking at him, I started to walk.

I was so close, I thought.

So close to taking back some small part of my life.

I could already feel it slipping away. But I couldn't quite put my finger on just what had gone wrong.

Other than…well, everything.

CHAPTER SIX

Time passes really fast when you don't want it to. Most of the time was spent on the computer, checking the various beaches, trying to figure out which one would work for me. I didn't *want* to leave *my* beach.

It felt like mine.

But I didn't see how I could go back there and face Jenks again.

He'd given me the first orgasm I'd had since my ex had all but torn my sexuality away, then I broke down and cried.

That's what happens when a woman is brutalized. Your sexuality is just…stolen. Things you enjoyed are taken away. My ex went a step further and took *everything*—light, sound, touch. There had been days when he'd left me alone down there, the food supply and the water dwindling away, and I'd wonder if I would be left alone to starve and die. Nobody would know. Nobody would care.

It hadn't been just my sexuality he'd stripped, but my very sense of self.

I'm taking those pieces of me back, or trying to.

I don't know how good of a job I'm doing, though, when the very first time a man brought me to climax it left me feeling so shaken, so shattered.

"And you're still planning on running away. Hiding."

As I studied the route to the beach I'd decided to check out, I acknowledged that I was doing just that. Running away. Hiding. And I knew why. If Jenks looked at me with that mix of pity and sympathy I'd grown used to seeing in the hospital, it would tear out another piece of my soul. I'd already lost too much. I don't know how much of me I can afford to lose.

He called me strong, but I wasn't.

Not really. It's a fight just to get out the door. Checking the locks, once, then again. Then going back up the stairs, because I'm *quite* certain I'd really checked them, but I wasn't positive.

Finally, I was sure so I let myself leave and it was just in time to see my shadow across the street come out. His eyes met mine and to my surprise, he jerked his gaze away, as if he didn't want me to notice him.

That was…new.

They'd never cared before. What had changed?

I didn't know and I hesitated, ready to duck back inside, but he cut to the left, heading down to the end of the street and disappearing around the corner. That wasn't right. The bus. He was supposed to get on the bus.

Maybe he was going to follow—

"Good morning."

My heart jumped up into my throat and I turned slowly and saw Jenks sitting on the low brick wall in front of my house. Two cups of coffee sat next to him. He had on his board shorts, a pair of sandals and his sunglasses. Nothing else.

Surprise stuttered in my chest as I stared at him, edging out of the ebb and flow of bodies, but still keeping my distance. Once I was about two feet away, I stopped, running my hand up and down the strap of my bag, shifting from one foot to the other.

"What… Why are you here?" I finally managed to ask.

He pushed his sunglasses up, his eyes resting on my face. "Well, I'm half afraid to answer that question because I think you're going to get mad at me, Shadow," he finally said.

I blinked. "Why am I going to get mad at you?"

"Because I'm sitting here waiting for you…and I know how you feel about that kind of thing." He said it bluntly, didn't offer any pretty lies or try to explain it away.

It made it a little easier to swallow, but yes, the uneasiness settled in my chest and grew. I looked down the street, my eyes seeking out the blue of the ocean, although I couldn't see it from here. I wanted my table. I wanted my sketchbooks. I wanted the peace and quiet I found only at the beach.

"Why are you waiting for me?" I had to force the question out.

"Because something told me you were going to cut and run, maybe find someplace else to spend your morning." This time his voice was soft, a little more hesitant, and I found myself looking back at him.

44

For the first time, I saw something nervous, almost vulnerable on his face.

I shouldn't let myself care.

Looking down at my feet, I didn't answer. And I told myself I didn't care.

"Were you?"

"It crossed my mind."

"Don't."

Closing my eyes, I tried not to let myself hear the soft plea in his words. Tried not to think about anything but what I needed to feel safer. Secure. Away from him, I'd find some measure of control again.

Although it was an illusion. I knew that. I'd thrown the word *safety* in his face. Nobody really knew how much of an illusion things like *safety* and *control* truly were.

A sigh shuddered out of me and I lifted my head, met his gaze. "Why?" I asked softly. "What does it matter to you?"

"Because I'd miss seeing you," he said. He climbed off the wall then and came to me. He lifted a hand to my cheek and the touch of his fingers, rough against my skin, sent sensation bolting through me. I'd relived the memory of that touch throughout the weekend. "If you need me to apologize for what happened, I'll do it. I didn't mean to make you—"

When I rose up to my toes to kiss him, I don't know who was more surprised.

Him.

Or me.

Slowly, I slid my hands up his chest, his skin hot and bare under my palms, smooth and steady and strong. It was another blistering shock against my senses, and in the back of my mind I could almost see myself arching against him, pulling my shirt away and seeing how it felt to be skin to skin.

His hand came up, cupped my hip.

I tensed.

He started to pull away.

I whispered, "No. Please…"

Some men might think that I wanted him to stop.

That was the very last thing I wanted.

Each touch, though, was a brutal agony. Almost more than I could handle, and I could handle a lot. Almost always pain, though. I'd rarely had the chance to experience pleasure and that was what this was—pure, excruciating pleasure, and all he was doing was kissing me, letting me feel his chest under my hands while his fingers curved around my hip and held me steady.

I eased closer and slid my hands farther up, looping my arms around his neck. It was nerve-racking, being so bold—and it felt terribly bold—but I wanted to feel that broad, heavy chest against my breasts.

When I finally did, I tore my mouth away and sucked in a breath.

And Jenks buried his face against my neck, his mouth brushing over my skin.

It took me a minute to realize he was talking, because every word sent a shiver racing through me.

Finally, though, I realized, and concentrated on his voice.

"Do you really have to find another spot, Shadow?"

He didn't tell me not to. If he had, I could have walked away. Maybe it would be *best* if I did walk away. Walking away was safer. Walking away protected me.

Walking away was *lonely.*

And now, it was no longer an option.

I'd let him inside and now I had to deal with it.

The idea wasn't as terrifying as it should have been.

In less than ten hours, I was going to have my first date in more than eight years.

I'd spent five years married to a monster. Three years trying to recover from that. And before my time in hell, there had been a whirlwind courtship.

The day I'd met my ex, he'd shown up at the art store, claiming he was interested in learning to paint, and instead of buying any acrylics or pastels, he'd spent thirty minutes flirting with me. He left with my phone number and my entire world changed over the next few months.

I went on a date with him two days after I met him.

Six months later, we were married.

It was eight and a half years ago, almost to the day.

And now, I was getting ready to go out on the first date since then.

Jenks had asked again. We'd been talking at the beach for over a month now.

He'd brought me to climax and then to tears, and every day since that night, if I went to the beach—*my* beach—he walked me home. Two days ago, he'd asked me if I was free on Friday.

Marla had called earlier in the week and asked if I could come over that night, but they would be delighted if I cancelled because I had a *date*.

I didn't know what he had planned.

And it didn't matter.

For the past two weeks, whenever I left to go to the beach, or anywhere else, I looked to see if the man my husband had hired was following me, but he never was.

Maybe my ex had set up somebody new.

Maybe he hadn't. I didn't know and I didn't care—

"I don't care."

I paused in the middle of chalking my hair. Stunned, I lowered the hair chalk and stared at my reflection, all but stupefied. "I don't care," I said again, all but dazed as I realized that.

Yes, if I saw the man, my emotions would change, but just then, I could think about it without that slippery, sliding fear festering inside me. This wasn't *my* sickness, wasn't my fault and I didn't have to let it control me.

More, it was time I did something about it.

No, I had no guarantee I was going to win. And maybe my ex had the money to pay people to watch me. But I wasn't exactly broke myself. If he could pay people, there was bound to be something I could do as well.

Something to think about, I decided.

Maybe I could get started now. A look at the clock told me I had plenty of time, and maybe it was a good way to spend the next few hours. Researching, losing myself in facts and data and information. Things that were concrete. As long as I didn't think about why I was digging into any of this—

The doorbell rang.

And then I didn't have time to think about anything because when I opened the door, the tall, willowy redhead standing on the other side caught me up in a tight hug and for a moment, I was so swept away in love, nothing else mattered.

"Hi, Marla."

"You're really going on a date."

I eyed Marla's reflection in the mirror before I shifted my attention back to the closet.

What in the world was I going to wear?

I hadn't had a date in so long. A date. Stroking a finger down the blue streak in my hair, I reached out and touched the sleeve of the poet blouse I'd been wearing. He told me he liked to unwrap me. But even though I loved all of the clothes I'd bought for myself, suddenly none of them worked.

"I need new clothes."

Marla arched her brows. Then she leaned forward and wrapped her arms around her knees. "Oh, honey. I thought you'd never get to this point. Just what time is this date?"

A quick glance at the clock had me grimacing. "Too soon." I couldn't pick out clothing in a short amount of time. It took me days, sometimes even weeks.

Groaning, I leaned my head against the mirror. "He's picking me up at eight."

Strong, slim arms came around me. "Do you trust me?" Marla asked.

"Trust you?" I cracked open an eye. "Well…"

She squeezed tighter. "Yes or no. Do you trust me?"

"Well… Yeah." *I think. Maybe. Mostly. I don't know.* I managed to keep most of that behind my teeth.

Marla laughed. Delighted, she said, "You trust me about as far as you can throw me, but that's okay. Honey, we are going shopping and this time, you're going to let me pick you out *one* dress. You can hem-haw over everything else, for weeks, if you have to, but for a date, this time, trust me. Okay?"

I didn't know if I liked the sound of that.

"You want to look absolutely smashing, completely unlike yourself for this date?" Marla asked, bending down and pressing her cheek to mine.

That, I thought, actually sounded nice.

"It's too short."

I shoved the dress back at her.

She refused to take it, her arms crossed over her chest, one red brow arched as she smirked at me. "You said you'd let me choose *one* outfit and then you could bitch about whatever else."

I stared at the dress, slightly horrified.

It was cuter than anything I'd ever seen, but I couldn't wear it.

A vintage piece—black and dotted with red cherries—it looked like something out of the fifties. Draped over Marla's arm was a red petticoat.

A sexy little number like that, a red petticoat. And she had a pair of red heels tucked up against the wall. How long had it been since I'd worn a pair of shoes like that?

"It's not too short. It falls about two inches above your knee, which is perfect for you. You don't want it too long—it won't flatter you. You want to show a little bit of leg." Then she flashed me a wicked grin. "Besides, think about how much *he* would hate it."

The knot in my throat had swelled to the size of a boulder and I could hardly breathe. Him.

Yes. Him.

Marla knew all about him.

One night, not long after Seth had told me they were serious, I'd told her about my ex. Warned her. Told her that he might try to go after her and she'd curled her lip. *Let him try,* she'd said. Then she'd admitted that Seth had already told her about him.

She didn't know much, but she knew enough and it was more than she wanted to know. More than I liked her knowing.

It had made it easier over the years, though, having that female confi-dante, somebody I could count on, somebody I could tell. She knew some of what he'd done. Some, not all. Nobody knew everything.

But it was easier, having her know *something.* She understood and I liked that.

She knew what it took for me to reach out and take that dress back, turn and hold it up to my chest, stare at my reflection in the mirror. She even understood how my hands trembled as I imagined how I'd look.

"You'll look amazing in it," she said quietly.

Maybe I would.

Swallowing the ache in my throat, I tried to find the *me* I'd been eight years ago, nine. Tried to think of how I'd been then. Before him. I would have looked at this dress. I might not have had the confidence then, but I would have looked…and longed for it. Wished for it.

My voice trembled as I whispered, "I'll try it on."

It took everything I had to do just that.

CHAPTER SEVEN

The shoes pinched my toes.

It was a weird thing to think about as I walked to the door. But if I was thinking about how those peep-toe platform heels pinched my toes, maybe I wouldn't think about how the neckline of the dress revealed so much of my boobs. Maybe I wouldn't think about the goose bumps breaking out on my skin and maybe I wouldn't think about how I was shaking inside.

A date.

A date with Jenks.

But then I opened the door and his eyes met mine, then dropped to roam over me and the goose bumps that had me shivering faded, replaced by a low, simmering heat that was just as unsettling, but oh, so much better.

I'd take that heat any day, especially when he moved in and reached up, touched his fingers to one of the blue streaks in my hair. "You look amazing," he murmured.

"I wasn't sure if you'd like it," I said, swallowing. "You said something about unwrapping me. This is…well. Different."

He chuckled and cupped my chin. "Unwrapping you. Undoing me. It's all the same," he murmured against my lips. "And I'm just about all undone here. Shadow…you dress however you want." He lifted his head just a little, eying me. "Did I pass the test?"

It hit me, then. Had I been testing him?

Unconsciously, maybe.

Along the way, I'd probably thrown a hundred tests in his path. He hadn't blinked when I'd shown him the art that had been my escape. Of course, neither had my ex...at the time.

Deep inside, a kernel of anger grew and as Jenks watched me, that kernel grew and grew until it was a flame, then a wildfire. His eyes lingered on me and I turned on my heel, storming inside the cozy, quiet place where I'd made myself a home. The locks beckoned me. Had I checked? Once, yes. Twice, yes.

I should check a third—

No.

So tired of this, so tired of the control he'd had on me.

"You're mad."

I shot him a look over my shoulder as I continued the check around my living room. The locks there were all good. He had to be quiet, because if he wasn't, I'd have to start all over. "I'm not mad."

I was furious, and I didn't even know why. No.

That was wrong. I *did* know why.

I was angry...*with myself.*

Angry because I still allowed this. Because I still *did* this. Slamming my hands down against the bookshelf lodged in front of the back door, I let out a small scream.

Hands came down on my shoulders.

"Shadow...what's wrong?"

Closing my eyes, I tried to keep the answer trapped inside. I was so close. I knew it. So close to falling apart. "Everything."

His lips touched my temple. "All of this because of a dress?"

"No." He managed to shock a laugh out of me. "All of this because I'm a mess, Jenks. I'm such a mess. He made me this way."

"No." His hands, rough and strong, smoothed down over my shoulders, bared by the halter-styled dress I wore. I hadn't left so much skin bared in years and his touch felt indescribably good. It almost brought tears to my eyes. I couldn't even begin to describe how amazing, what it did to me to feel his hands skimming across me, how it sent my heart skittering around in my chest, the way my blood heated, how my skin seemed as though it was two sizes too small. "He didn't *make* you anything. He tried to tear you down, but you survived. You're still here. And tonight's supposed to be ours, right? Why let him in?"

He pressed his lips to the skin behind my ear and I gasped.

Sensation—too much.

I couldn't handle it.

Then he added more to it, grabbing the hem of my skirt and placing his hand on my knee, stroking up, forcing the material of my dress and petticoat higher as he went. "If you're going to let anybody in, can't it be me?" he teased, catching my earlobe between his teeth and tugging.

A jolt echoed through me.

Slowly, he guided me around and I fell into the heat of his gaze, fell into the heat of him as he backed me into the wall.

His mouth brushed against mine. "You have no answer," he whispered, his tongue tracing the line of my mouth.

Oh, I had all kinds of answers. The problem was that I couldn't put them into words.

Part of me wanted to grab the material of my skirt and drag it up, then pull him against me.

Part of me wanted to push him out into the hallway so I could tuck myself away in my bed, rock myself while I thought and brooded and worried.

And the other part of me was just thinking I thought too much.

Tracing my hands down the hard, muscled line of his chest, I plucked at the hem of his shirt and then slid my hands under it. What would it be like, I wondered, to have the freedom to just *be*?

To give in to this burning, aching *need* and not worry about the fear.

The power to do that was right there.

Turning my face into his neck, I breathed in the scent of his skin. Salt, surf, man. Jenks. I wanted this, him, so much.

His hands moved to my hips and tugged, bringing me in contact with his body and I groaned at the feel of him against me. "Have you ever wanted something so bad, but been afraid to reach out? And even if you *wanted* to reach out, you didn't know how?" I asked, the words muffled against his skin.

He stroked a hand up my back. "I've been wanting something pretty fucking bad for the past few months," he said, his voice gruff. "And yeah, I've been afraid to do anything about it, because one wrong move is going to ruin it." He rubbed his cheek against mine. "What's the wrong move here, sugar? Do I move back? We can go out to dinner, catch a movie. I can come back another day…"

I pushed him back.

My heart thudded in my ears, roaring like a lion as I stared into his eyes.

The wrong move.

After an entire lifetime of them, it seemed like I should be able to recognize the wrong move easily enough.

But it wasn't as easy as one might think.

If the wrong move was reaching out to grab the hem of his shirt and drag it up, would I hear warning bells?

I don't know, but I did that, and I did it slowly, listening for said alarm bells.

There were none. Just the roaring in my ears.

My hands trembled as I unbuttoned his shirt. Once it hung open, framing his chest, I paused, stroking my hands along the muscled plane. I leaned in, pressed my lips to the middle of his chest, felt his heart pounding hard and fast. He cupped the back of my head and I thought I felt a tremor rack him. A rush of need, a rush of emotion and yearning and warmth and wonder crashed through me.

I didn't want to feel like that.

It frightened me.

But there was no stopping it.

My hands fell away and Jenks lifted his head, staring at me, the velvet of his eyes intense, hot as molten chocolate, lingering on my face before dropping to rest on my mouth. "I want to kiss you," he said, his voice blunt and uncompromising.

"Then do it."

Maybe if I let him take control here, I could handle this better. It wasn't a scary thing if I *wanted* him to take control, right?

One hand stroked up my middle, stopping on my neck, just under my chin, and he angled my head back, lowered his until his mouth was just a breath away. "Do it?" he whispered. "Just like that? What about our date?"

"Maybe I want this to be the date," I said, forcing the words out of my tight throat. "Or maybe we can do this, then go out."

He laughed, rubbing his lips over mine. "Sugar, if this keeps up, the only thing I'm going to feel like doing is getting horizontal with you."

I blinked at him, my heart jumping up to lodge in my throat. Horizontal. With Jenks. The idea didn't bother me at all.

"Or maybe vertical…" He caught one of my legs, dragging me open and leaning in against me. "Right like this would be just about perfect."

My breath froze as I felt him rock against me, the silk of my panties gliding back and forth.

And the sensation was too much, way, way too much.

My nails bit into his shoulders as I clutched him against me. "Dillian…"

He sank his teeth into my lower lip.

And I climaxed, right there.

"*That*," he growled. "That is just about perfect."

And the best part was…I didn't even cry.

Although a few minutes later, part of me wanted to. Cry, or maybe pull out my hair. Hit something. Kick something.

I just wanted to be normal. If I was a normal, healthy female, I could be in bed with Jenks right now. Instead, he was smoothing my dress down around my hips, even as I tried to tug him back to me.

Finally, he caught my hands and guided them up to his chest. The look in his eyes was caught between frustration and need and he said, "Enough, Shadow. Enough, okay?"

"Why?" The question tore out of my dry throat, my voice rusty, as if it had been months since I'd used it. Edgy, I pushed him away and stormed over to the pretty kitchen I rarely used and opened the refrigerator. I had bottled water in there. I could only drink bottled water anymore and it had to be Aquafina.

It was just another one of those stupid little quirks I'd developed. The cop who had hustled me into his car that night I'd escaped from hell had some water in his car and he'd given me the bottle. It was the first time I had been given anything other than tepid, stale water in months and the doctors who had examined me thought it had been almost two days since I'd had anything to drink. Severe dehydration, severe malnutrition.

The taste of that water sliding down my throat had been the sweetest thing I could remember. I'd live. I tasted that water and I'd realized I was free. Each time I held one of those silly plastic bottles, it reaffirmed that belief. I was alive.

Now, my hands shook as I unscrewed the cap and lifted the bottle to my lips. I downed half of it before I slid him a look from the corner of my eye. "Why is it enough? I thought…"

Then I stopped speaking, blowing out a slow breath.

I needed to stop thinking. Every time I did, I was wrong anyway.

His boots scuffed against the floor and the compulsion to look up at him was strong, but I didn't. I continued to stare at the rust-colored walls of my kitchen. The stove and refrigerator were set against one wall and that wall was brick. I loved the rustic look of it, tried to imagine myself cooking in here. There had been a time when I'd enjoyed cooking. But that was that old life. That old me. The girl who had died in that forsaken hell.

"You thought what?"

Closing my eyes, I carefully screwed the top back on the water bottle. If I was quiet, if I didn't answer him, he'd get the point and just leave. I wouldn't have to humiliate myself. I wouldn't have to lay it out like that and embarrass myself.

His hands came down on my shoulders and the flinch escaped me before I could stop it. "When was the last time you had sex, sugar?" he asked.

That blunt, uncompromising question startled me into looking at him and his gaze was just as direct, just as unyielding as the question had been. Blood rushed to my face and I wanted to turn away, hide from him, but he didn't let me.

"When?" he asked again and those dark, penetrating eyes of his seemed to stare deep into my soul.

"Sex…" I murmured, looking away from him. It was easier to look at something other than his chest as I answered, I decided. "I haven't been with anybody since my marriage. I left him three years ago."

"And when was the last time you really slept with him?"

Something about that question, the way he phrased it, bothered me. Squirming out of his grasp, I turned away and put the water bottle back inside the refrigerator. There were twenty-one bottles—well, twenty now that I had opened one. Time to order another case of water. I drank three bottles a day. I recycled religiously and some part of me felt bad about the waste, but I couldn't drink the water from the tap. I'd tried the expensive filters and they just weren't the same.

It's weird how being deprived of something so simple can make such an impact on you.

"My husband liked sex," I said, forcing the words out.

"Did he now?" Jenks said, his voice soft, almost gentle. "So you liked making love with him."

The laugh was a harsh echo in the room and I spun around, the sneer on my face alien. "Oh, I didn't say that. I think we stopped…" The words tangled on my tongue. "*Making love* within six months of getting married. But he damn well forced me to have sex with him on a regular basis."

"If he forced you, then it wasn't sex." He crossed the floor, reaching up to cup my cheek once he was near. His touch was gentle. The look in his eyes was anything but. "There's a word for that, and I think you know what it is."

Tears stung my eyes. I couldn't stop them as they fell. "What do you want from me?"

"I just wanted an answer." He wrapped me up in his arms, a sigh drifting from him. His hand cupped the back of my head and I buried my face against his shirt. It felt so good to stand there. Just right there. I could happily do that, just that, for an eternity. "I don't want to hear what he did to you until you're ready to talk. And if that's never, then I can handle that."

"Then why are you asking about my fucking sex life?" I demanded, curling my fingers into the soft, silky material of his shirt.

He laughed softly, turning his face into my neck. His lips brushed against my ear and despite the turmoil inside me, I couldn't deny the pleasure that skittered through me at that light touch. "Because, sugar, if you and I end up horizontal, there are certain things to take into consideration, and I didn't come here planning to get you naked. At least not yet. But you don't go climbing into bed with somebody without protection. I didn't bring any. Do you have something here?"

It was a sign of just how out of touch I am that it took a minute for all of that to connect. I'd been with others before my marriage, but that had been a long time ago. So long. And once I'd gotten married...well, a woman doesn't need condoms to sleep with her husband. My cheeks went red as I eased back to shoot him a glance. "You mean..." I felt like an idiot. I took birth control but there were other considerations and it wasn't like we'd had *that* talk. "No. Ah...no. I don't have anything."

His thumb stroked my nape. "Okay, then." He turned us around and I found myself pinned between him and the counter. It wasn't a bad place to be. Not at all. My lids lowered as he rocked against me and some of that turmoil I carried inside melted away. "Here's what I think. I think we should go out on that date. See what happens. If you're still feeling... friendly...we can find a store. Take care of this little matter that's interfering. Then we can go to my place."

At those words, I tensed. His place.

"Why your place?" I asked and I had to squeeze the words out—jagged pieces of twisted, rusty iron that tore at my throat.

"Because everything you have here is a reminder." He nuzzled my neck. "It's a reminder of what you escaped, or a reminder of what he tried to make you into. It's a reminder of your freedom. Don't get me wrong, baby. I'm glad you have that, but for this one thing, I want nothing between us, around us, near us. I just want us."

CHAPTER EIGHT

The seafood place down on the water was one I'd want to try.
I'd just never gotten around to it. It wasn't the kind of restaurant you dropped into for a casual lunch on your own, and I never left home alone in the evening unless I was with Seth or Marla. Seth was still struggling to get through school. Marla was a dance instructor. They didn't have the kind of funds for this. I could do it, but even though always tried to handle it, they took their turn on paying for pizza and they insisted on taking their turn when it came to movie night. They definitely weren't going to let me take them to a place like Alistair's.

Tablecoths gleamed in the candlelight and music played softly in the background. The serving staff wore all black, save for the simple white aprons around their hips.

It was beautiful inside.

And for one, breath-sucking minute, I thought I caught a glimpse of my ex.

I stood there as the waiter pulled out my chair and my legs wouldn't move. I couldn't even lower myself to the seat and Jenks came to my side, touched my arm. "What's wrong?"

The sound of his voice broke the thick, awful hold of fear, but I still had a nasty taste in the back of my mouth as I forced myself to sit down. "I'm fine. Go…sit."

He did, but not without moving the seat first. He slid it around until it was angled closer to mine. The server said nothing, just moved the silverware and napkin and smiled.

"Would you like to see the wine list?" she asked as Jenks settled into his seat.

I barely managed to keep from saying, "Hell, yes."

"I would, yes." I was pleased to hear that my voice didn't shake. That was good.

As she made a discreet exit, Jenks leaned back in his seat and caught me with his gaze. "What's wrong?"

Fidgeting, I picked up the napkin and started to toy with the edges. "I…" I shot him a look and then slid my gaze over to the corner where I saw the dark-haired man. It could be him, I realized. It had been months since I'd seen him.

The hair style was different, but only slightly.

He wasn't wearing a suit, but here in the laid back, coastal Carolina town, that wasn't really odd. He would probably try to blend.

It really *could* be him.

My hands started to shake. My heart hammered and throbbed so hard I almost felt ill.

Why would he be here?

But I already knew the answer.

The answer sat next to me, so close I could feel the heat from his muscled thigh. Jenks had scared off one of his spies and he had to find another one, and more, he had to freak me out while he did it. I had to pay the price for slipping his leash.

A hand, strong and warm, covered mine. "Shadow, it's time to stop trying to handle all this fear by yourself."

Was it?

Could I trust anybody else with this?

From the corner of my eye, I caught movement and I looked up at the server as she appeared with the wine list. Automatically, I skimmed it and without batting a lash, my gaze shot straight down to the list of ports and dessert wines. Tapping on the one that looked the most appealing, I said, "Can you bring a bottle of this?"

She arched a brow. "Now or when you have dessert?"

"Now. I don't like reds or whites." And I needed a fucking drink.

Especially if I had to keep staring at the back of that dark head and wonder if it was him.

He'd like that, I thought. He'd like to make me wonder, and wait, and worry. It was so like him.

Once we were alone again, I looked at Jenks and blew out a breath. Then I angled my head to the table across the room. "The dark-haired man sitting with the older guy. I think it might be my ex."

Jenks had his elbows propped on the edge of the table and as I said those words, the muscles in his biceps went tight, the veins standing out in stark relief. His eyes skimmed the room, landed on the men in question, and then came back to me. "Why would he be here?"

I smiled sourly. "With him, the question is...why wouldn't he be?"

We lapsed into silence as the server brought out the wine and a few minutes later, I had my drink and we were left to ourselves again. Jenks had told her we'd let her know when we were ready to order. At the rate I was going, I just might not eat. Ever.

This had been a sucker punch of a day, that was for certain. Haltingly, I told him, "I can't tell you what it was like, what he did to me when we were married. Not yet, and definitely not when we're in public. I..." I took a sip of the wine, closed my eyes at the rush of sweetness, enjoyed the flavor of it as it broke across my taste buds before I swallowed. Then I put the glass down and clenched my trembling hands together. Looking at him, I forced myself to go on. "I never had anxiety before. Once I was... away, I developed OCD and I have panic attacks. All because of what he did to me. If I try to talk about it in public, I'll come apart, I know I will. Maybe one day I can tell you. I don't know. But he would come down here—he *has* come down here—just to let me know he's still there. That he can show up whenever he pleases. The day I left the hospital, he called, even though the hospital was told to block all calls from him. He called from a line at work, had managed to charm one of the nurses into putting the call through. He told me that I'd never be free of him. This is his little way of reminding me."

Seconds passed and then Jenks reached for the ice water the server had poured. He drained it, thunked it down on the table with enough force that several heads turned our way. I didn't care. In all honesty, I could have used the physical outlet myself. Broken something, maybe broken the wine bottle over somebody's skull.

"If you had the chance to make him disappear, would you take it?"

The question caught me off guard.

I stared at him, saw the glitter in his eyes. I pondered the question. If I could make him disappear...

I opened my mouth to answer, unsure of what I would say.

The answer surprised even me.

"I don't know. I don't want him hurting anybody, not ever again." I stared out the window, mesmerized by the rippling, rolling waters of the ocean. Then I slid my eyes back to look at Jenks. "I don't think I would, though. Some part of me wants to believe that some day, he'll pay for what he's done. That he'll have to sit in jail and answer for everything he did to me. For what he's done to other women."

Jenks' eyes narrowed. "Others."

"I'm not the first." Shaking my head, I continued my study of the ocean. "He has a taste for hurting people. He was...*good* at it. I can't believe it happened overnight. I don't know of anybody directly, but I can't be the only one."

He reached across the table and caught my free hand. "Do you want to leave?"

We could do that. He'd understand.

I wouldn't, though. I'd told myself I was going to start to live, let myself feel more. And if I left this place just because there was a man who may or may not be my ex-husband, I was going to regret it. I'd regret it for a very long time.

I took another sip of the wine. Let it linger in the mouth as I put the glass down. Then, without looking at Jenks, I reached for the menu.

My ex stopped controlling me when I let the fear stop controlling my life.

I had to take the reins. I couldn't do that by letting the fear run things for me.

Nearly an hour later, Jenks' eyes were hard and flat.

And a shiver raced down my spine. I guess I didn't need to look at the point. The way my body reacted was telling me everything I needed to know. But some part of me had to look.

The wine had me feeling pleasantly buzzed and maybe it even gave me a little bit of false confidence. I needed it, needed that warm little boost in my belly as I turned my head, casually glanced over. He was staring at me. Talking to the man he'd had dinner with, but staring at me.

"Don't keep staring at him," Jenks said, his voice low.

I couldn't look away. I felt like I'd been caught in the stare of a cobra, only this snake was so much more deadly. So much worse.

A snake could kill, yes. But it did it for instinctive reasons. For food, for protection.

A hand touched mine and I tore my gaze away, looked at Jenks.

His gaze was solemn. His fingers laced with mine and I gripped his hand as though it was the only thing that kept me from drowning. Drowning in a sea of fear, misery and death. That darkness swarmed up to grab me. I remembered it. I'd been thrown down inside a room where there was no light, no sound. Where I couldn't touch anything but the bare walls and my own body as I wasted away over the months. There was nothing else, and after a period of time, there was nobody else.

"The guy with him is walking away," Jenks said quietly. "But he's coming over here. I want to put him through the pavement. But if I do that, I'm going to get arrested and I'm not leaving you."

The grip I had on his hand turned almost desperate. "As much as I'd love to see him go through the pavement, I don't want you leaving me, either."

Then we didn't have time for anything else.

My skin went icy cold and I looked up, found myself staring into the wintry blue eyes of Stefan Stockman. Three years ago, I'd been known to the world as Grace Stockman, the young, sometimes awkward bride of the older, indulgent Boston blueblood.

His family was one of the oldest in Massachusetts. He'd broken the mold, though. Instead of being a lawyer like the rest of them, he'd chosen to open an art gallery and he did what he called *nurturing young talent...* that was how he'd found me.

Found me, fallen in love with me, married me. That was the fairy tale he'd told his family and the world.

I was his awkward, blushing bride, twenty when we said our vows. He had been thirty-five and he'd completely dazzled me.

Dazzled...maybe *blinded* is more like it.

Now, years later, as he stopped beside our table, I wondered how I ever could have missed the coldness I saw in him now.

I saw the flicker of disgust in his eyes as he looked me over. The girl I'd been, the girl who'd married him wanted to cringe, hide away, do something to please him and take that look away so he wouldn't hurt me.

The women I wanted to be was angry.

She wanted to hurt him—wanted to make him angrier, wanted to lash out and do something.

Where I found the courage, I don't know. Maybe it was the way Jenks rubbed his thumb across my skin, or the way he sat there, so calm and steady—or maybe it was the way he'd mentioned that he hoped my ex was dead in a ditch, and when I'd said he wasn't, Jenks had just calmly asked, *Do you want him to be?*

I don't know, but something gave me the courage and I pulled my hand from Jenks' steady grasp and reached for the bottle of wine. Only a small amount remained and I poured it into my glass, every last drop, and then I leaned back in my chair, lifting the wine to my lips before I met Stefan's cold gaze.

"Did you need something?" I asked. My voice wasn't level. And the words weren't as carefree as I'd hoped.

But I'd said it.

I'd all but dared him.

Three years, five years ago, that would have resulted in a blow that would leave me on the floor, probably bleeding, most definitely gasping for air.

He wouldn't dare strike me here.

It didn't mean I wasn't terrified.

And the son of a bitch knew it.

But I'd pissed him off. I saw the flicker in his eyes and that angry woman inside me wanted to dance in victory. I appeased her with another sip of wine.

"Grace. Lovely to see you looking so...sane," he murmured. "Are you still taking your medication?"

The wine was a cool, welcome relief down my throat, but there wasn't enough of it. I needed more, needed another entire bottle. Tossing it back was tempting, but I didn't let myself. I savored one more sip and put it down. As I glanced over at the table, I saw Jenks' hand. As though he'd felt my gaze, he brushed his fingers over mine.

I turned my hand up and he twined our fingers together.

The sight of that steadied me enough that I could look back at Stefan and respond. "I sort of stopped needing meds once I was away from you."

The words were just a ghost of sound.

Still, he heard me.

I heard the soft *hmmmm* he made under his breath. He started to reach out his hand—he was so clever with his touches. The man could inflict pain and everybody else would see nothing but a loving brush of a hand, a supportive gesture.

I recoiled, desperate to get away.

But he never had a chance to so much as touch my hair.

Jenks broke our grip, uncoiled from his chair and slid between us. He moved like the ocean, powerful and unstoppable.

My breath hitched in my chest as he placed a staying hand on Stefan's chest, keeping him from moving any closer to me.

"Hands to yourself, my friend," he advised, his voice low, gentle. But the sound of it sent a shudder down my spine.

"You should watch yourself," Stefan said. "I was just having a word with my wife."

"The last I heard, you two were divorced. And it doesn't matter. I see her pulling back, so unless she *asks* for you to touch her, you *don't touch her*." Jenks took a step toward him and he towered over Stefan.

Stefan was fit—with his gym-sculpted muscles and his perfect manicures and his hair that was cut every three weeks, at precisely 4:45, by the same girl. Once she'd been ill with the flu and Stefan had harangued the salon owner so scathingly, the man had sent him flowers the next day to make up for the technician's *lapse in judgment*.

Over the flu.

I'd never seen Stefan back away from anybody.

Until that moment.

Jenks crowded into him, looking even larger, and Stefan backed up. He regretted it the minute he did it. I saw it in his eyes. But he couldn't undo that one silent step in retreat, either.

He smoothed his sleeves down, made it look as though he'd done it intentionally before he slid me a look. "You went and found yourself a devoted toy this time, my dear."

My heart slammed in my throat. That was the lie he'd liked to use during the divorce proceedings. He loved me and wanted to make our marriage work—it didn't matter that I'd had numerous lovers and one of them must have kidnapped me, badly abused me during the months I'd been missing—and how he had searched for me. Those were the lies he'd told.

Something twisted inside me. People had believed him. While I stood there with bruises, as I struggled to learn how to eat all over again, they had looked at me and wondered.

My breathing hitched and I darted a look at Jenks from the corner of my eye. He was staring at Stefan as though he was in the mood to crack open the man's skull and play with whatever contents he found inside. The gruesome image steadied me a little.

How steady could I be, though, sitting there, so close to the man who had tortured me? Imprisoned me?

I reached for the glass of wine.

"Still drinking too much, Grace? You think that will help your situation?"

Curling my fingers into a fist, I started to pull my hand back. I hated myself in that moment and made myself grab the glass, tossing it back and glaring at my ex.

"You think talking is going to help *yours?*" Jenks asked, his voice a silken, low drawl.

As Jenks glared down at my husband, I caught sight of the server, standing just a few feet from our table. She had a nervous look on her face and when she caught my gaze, she rushed over.

"Is there a problem?" she asked, pitching her voice low, directly to me. "Can you—"

Stefan interrupted. "I'm just having a conversation with my wife," Stefan said, cutting us off. "You can go."

I held her gaze. People had asked me, before, during that old life, if I needed help. If things were okay. *If there was a problem.* If I'd been honest then, if I'd had the courage…if I'd *tried*, maybe it wouldn't have been so bad. I'd never know. But I'd be damned if I was silent now.

"He's not my husband," I said, forcing my voice loud enough to be heard. "I divorced him three years ago and I'd rather him *not* be here." I licked my lips and then I continued to speak. "Yes. Yes, there's a problem."

People had been trying to ignore us, but at those words, a few of them stopped pretending. I saw one woman lean over to her husband and he pushed his chair back a few inches, eying Jenks and Stefan.

The server straightened and looked at my ex.

"Sir, as you're not dining with them, please leave them to enjoy their dinner."

He stared at her, his eyes narrowing.

She held his gaze.

I wished I had that courage.

The man who'd been watching the tableau a few tables away started to rise.

But at that moment, Stefan turned and walked away, his carriage perfect, his steps unhurried. At the door, he paused and looked back at me. A small smile curved his lips. This wasn't over. He wouldn't let it be over, not as easily at that.

Wilting against the back of my chair, I started to shake.

And then abruptly, I bolted out of the seat and practically ran to the restroom. I barely made it before I emptied my stomach. The lovely dinner Jenks had bought me came up in one violent spasm after another.

A hand brushed the back of my neck.

I didn't have to look to know who it was.

How was it that he always managed to be around when I was at my worst? Straightening away from the porcelain toilet, I rested my head against his chest. "You shouldn't be in here."

"Yeah, well. I don't figure they are going to arrest me because my girl-friend got sick and I didn't want her to be alone," he murmured, stroking my hair back from my cold, damp face.

"Your girlfriend."

"*Hmmm.*" He stroked a paper towel back from my face. "I've had my hand inside your panties and you drew dirty pictures of me. I think that counts for something. You ready to get up, sugar?"

I didn't know if I could.

My legs were weak, wobbly and the thought of getting upright, walking back out there in front of people was just more than I could handle.

But I couldn't stay there on my ass, sprawled against his chest in the middle of the ladies room either. "I'm going to have to walk out there, aren't I?" I asked.

"At some point." He rubbed his thumb down my arm and said, "I left some cash on the table. The bill is paid. We can just leave once you're ready."

Eyes closed, I breathed in his scent and then opened my eyes. It would be a good idea to get ready now, before anybody else came into the restroom. We wouldn't be alone much longer. And I couldn't handle the idea of trying to explain any of this away. "Let's get up," I said, taking a deep breath and trying to brace myself.

I didn't even come close, but just like that, I was on my feet and Jenks was the one bracing me, his hands on my waist, his eyes studying my face. "You want to wash your face?" He brushed my hair back and I nodded.

I'd wash my face, my hands…I'd wash my entire body right there in the sink if I thought I could get away with it.

"Let's do this so I can go home," I whispered. I just wanted to collapse and hide. Forget this day had happened.

That was all I wanted.

▲▼▲

The little cottage I found myself in front of was *not* my home.

It was cute.

It was quaint.

But it wasn't my home.

Swallowing, I looked over Jenks.

"This isn't home."

He stroked a hand down my back.

"He knows where you live, doesn't he?"

That was one thing I hadn't even considered. Stefan did know where I lived. He knew about my job, he knew where I shopped. Up until tonight, I'd had only one secret—Jenks.

Resisting the need to press myself against him, I pulled back and wrapped my arms around myself. "Why are we here?"

"Because if he doesn't know about this place, he can't look for you here. And I'm not keen on the idea of him knowing where you sleep. All he has to do is hang out at the bar across the way, watch for you." He touched his thumb to my lip. "I could take you home, just sleep on your couch. But I'll be honest, I want you here. In my bed. I want you safe and I want you away from anything that has to do with him."

It sounded so simple.

So easy.

He stroked his hands down my arms and then dipped his head, murmured into my ear. "I also want to take you inside, strip you out of this dress, maybe leave you wearing that petticoat while I spread you out across my bed. It faces the ocean and we can open the windows. We can listen to the waves while I make you come."

His voice was a low, steady stroke across my skin and I reached down and back, gripped his hips to steady myself. Against my flesh, I could feel the cool night air. He dipped his head and I shivered as his lips brushed against my shoulder. His hair touched my cheek and I could smell the shampoo he'd used. My head spun. Too much sensation.

"Will you come inside with me, Shadow?" he asked, and nuzzled my neck just below my ear. Then he caught the lobe between his teeth and tugged.

I felt it echo through every inch of me.

"Yes."

It really wasn't much of a question, what I'd do. Not really.

CHAPTER NINE

His bedroom opened up onto a deck, a tiny little U. Both the bedroom and the deck faced the water and although the night wasn't cold, he built a fire in the fire pit and I sat down in front of it, surprised at how good the heat felt against my skin.

Behind us, the bedroom was lit by the soft, golden glow of a few carefully placed lamps. There was a massive painting over the bed. The images in it looked like the mermaid he'd shown me.

There was something familiar about it, but I couldn't place it and it had been ages since I'd really spent much time looking at art. The years of my marriage, I hadn't been able to and then it had become a vicious, almost painful reminder.

Another piece of myself I needed to take back.

A bottle of Aquafina was put in front of me. I shot him a look. He sat down in the seat on the other side of the fire pit, holding a bottle of beer in his hands. "You have a shitload of that water in your fridge," he said. "I figured you must like it, so I bought some to keep." He shrugged, looked down. "Just in case. Figured you might need it."

Reaching for the bottle, I twisted the top off and took a drink, then another. My throat was painfully dry. And it would get worse.

I thought maybe I needed to tell him.

Everything.

Before.

He might not want me after he knew. If that was going to happen, I needed to know. It would be easier to just never know what could be, then to tell him later and lose him. Maybe it wouldn't be as bad as it had been when I'd been locked away in that tight, dark basement, alone with nothing but my own voice, my own fears, but I'd be alone again. Nobody had been able to get inside the walls I'd built around me like Jenks had. I didn't want to let him any further inside unless I knew I could trust him to stay.

Nervously, I twisted the bottle around and around in my hands, staring at the flames through it while I tried to figure out where to start.

The beginning. That was where the cops had always told me to start. They wanted to know when the beatings, the abuse had started.

But it went farther back than that.

"I was going to be an art major," I said softly, staring into the flames. "That was how I met him…"

Nervous, I glanced at him, saw that he was staring at nothing else. It was like I was all that existed for him.

And that gave me the courage to continue.

"I was going to leave him. That was when he…"

I had no idea how long I'd been talking.

My throat was raw, raspy. My eyes were swollen and they itched.

There was a box of Kleenex, mostly empty, and a wastebasket, almost full.

And I sat on Jenks' lap now.

His arms held me loosely. More than once I'd gotten up to pace, but always, I came back there. Part of me thought I'd have to bolt as I came to this part, but now, as I tried to force the words out, I just started to shake.

I couldn't say it.

I couldn't even think about it.

Nervous, I pushed away from him and scrambled for my phone.

Stefan had hated the fact that the cops felt they had enough to push for an investigation. That meant certain things were on record. At times, reading through those records—*public* records—was the only thing that grounded me and made me remember that I was out. I'd gotten out.

That I hadn't gone crazy and that he hadn't been able to cover all his lies with *more* lies.

Some people *knew*.

There were times, when the despair got to be too much, I found some small sliver of strength by looking at the few articles that *had* gotten published. There wasn't much. The Stockman family was a powerful one and they'd managed to silence so much of the information.

But there was one article that might do what I couldn't just then.

With shaking hands, I got my phone and opened the *iBooks* app and found the PDF.

Then I shoved it into his hands and clambered away.

I didn't have to read it.

I knew it, almost word for word.

Boston's Son, Stefan Stockman—Abuser or Victim?

Stefan Stockman has been accused of horrible crimes that seem to have been ripped straight out of a psychological thriller. Grace Stockman, his wife, was found wandering the streets in the hours after the tornado that killed eight people. She had been missing for nine months.

An extensive search revealed nothing.

Mr. Stockman had offered rewards for any clue leading to her disappearance, but none of the information led to her discovery.

The officer who found Mrs. Stockman said she stumbled into the street, "looking like a war refugee". While the hospital will give no information, sources reveal that she has had multiple bones broken and will need extensive surgery to repair the damage done to her face.

The accused in this case is her husband, Stefan Stockman. Our sources reveal that she has told the Boston Police Department that she was held against her will in the basement of a house destroyed during the March 22 tornado and that was what had allowed her to escape. During those months, she reports she was raped repeatedly, beaten, and often starved.

There has been no comment from the Stockman family, but the law firm retained by Mr. Stockman assures us that he is innocent and that Mrs. Stockman underwent a horrifying experience at the hands of an abusive lover. Her husband claims will be there to support her as she recovers.

The sound of the phone being placed on the table was horribly loud. It wasn't, not really. But just then, the sound of a pin dropping might have shattered me.

"How long did this go on?" he asked quietly.

I looked at him blankly. "How long was I trapped?" I frowned, trying to think.

But he shook his head. "How long did you...were you...how long did he hurt you?"

"A lifetime," I whispered. "And he's still doing it." Shivering, I thought about the basement. Jenks wrapped his arm around me. "Years, though. It went on for years. It started almost right after I married him. It was June when I told him I was leaving him—I told him in the morning and he left for work without saying a word. I went to a hotel and lay down to sleep." Haunted, wanting to scream, I shifted my eyes to Jenks and focused on his face. I was *here*, I was *safe*. "Then I woke up in the basement. It was days before I even realized he was the one who'd taken me. There were no lights. It was completely dark. He'd painted over the windows and he only came over at night." My voice had faded down to a whisper. "Lights hurt my eyes for days after. Now I can't stand the dark."

I looked back at the phone, vaguely aware of Jenks as he started to pace. Then, as something shattered, I flinched, biting back a scream.

Jenks stood there by at the end of the couch.

There was a wet spot on the wall, and the shards of glass, all that remained from the bottle of beer he'd been drinking, lay on the ground below it.

"Fuck," he muttered, following the direction of my eyes. "I'm sorry, Shadow. Sorry... I just..."

He turned away, his shoulders rising, falling on a ragged breath.

I just shook my head and turned back to the ocean. One might think that violent outbursts like that would freak me out, especially with Stefan's proclivity to violence. But even when he beat me, he never lost control. He would break my arm and smile as he did it.

I'd rather see some outburst, some expression of anger any day.

It was the lack of emotion that scared me more than anything.

Shivering, I ran my hands up and down my arms.

"You saw nobody, nothing, that entire time?"

"Stefan would come. But I never saw him. He'd grab me, push me down..." I rubbed the back of my neck. The memory of my hair, how he'd twist it around his hands like a rope and use it to pen me in place made me want to vomit. And I had. I'd done that. There had been times I'd lie there, on the floor, choking on my own vomit as he hurt me. All I had wanted was to die. And Stefan wouldn't give me that.

"It said there was a tornado?"

Closing my eyes, I nodded. "It destroyed the house. Eight people died. I was able to get out. I saw lightning. It..." I forced my lashes up, stared at the sky. "It had been so long since I'd seen light, I thought I was going crazy. And I was weak, so weak. He'd bring food. Peanut butter, crackers. Old bread. Awful stuff. And a bucket of water. I had to use that to drink and wash myself. There was a toilet and shower, but the showerhead stopped working after a few months. He hadn't been there in a few days and I'd run out of food. Then water. I was so weak, I could barely walk, but I saw the lightening and I realized that was my chance. Maybe my only chance. It was so hard to leave."

"Why?"

Turning, I stared at him. "He could have been waiting," I said simply. "To trick me. To see if I'd try. If he was…"

Then I shook my head, blocking out that thought. I couldn't think of that. It did no good, now. And he hadn't been waiting. Stefan had gone to Chicago for a show and the storm had grounded his plane. That had freed me. He hadn't had any chance at all to stop me. All of his arrogance, all the control he had over me, and all it had taken was Mother Nature.

And a cop with a bottle of Aquafina.

"There was a cop. He lived two streets over and was out because of the storm. He saw me, yelled at me. I didn't understand what he was saying. It had been so long since I'd heard anything. Stefan hadn't even spoken to me the last few months. He'd just…" I stopped, plucked at my shirt. He knew, didn't he? He'd said as much. "He would rape me. Beat me. But he never said a word. All of it in silence. I saw nothing, I heard nothing. All I could do was feel and all I could feel was pain. And then I was free. On the street while the rain was still coming down and there's this cop, staring at me like I'm crazy. He sees the bruises left over—Stefan had beaten me badly the last time. Maybe a week earlier. And my face…" I touched my cheekbone. It wasn't noticeable now, but it had been crooked then. "My face was wrong. He'd hit me, broken the bones in my face and they didn't heal right. The cop knew something was wrong. Nine months in hell and all it took to get me out was a storm. Eight people died, Jenks."

The strength drained out of me and I went to the floor. "Eight people died, but I made it out of hell. Why did it happen that way?"

A moment later, I was wrapped in his arms. He kissed my cheek and started to rock me. "It just did. It was a tornado. It could have killed you just as easily. Don't go taking that weight on when you already have enough horror inside you." His chest rumbled against my back as he spoke. I wanted to take comfort in his words, but I didn't know if I could. If I should.

We sat like that. Staring out over the dark water of the Atlantic. I lost track of how much time passed.

Then he reached up and pushed my hair back, pressed his cheek to mine.

"Why, for fuck's safe, isn't he in jail?"

"They declined to prosecute. It was my word against his and he'd had already painted me as this…unstable woman who had issues with alcohol and depression. His friends backed him up. They…" I bit my inner cheek and looked up at the ceiling until the ache faded. "In the end, a few cops believed me, but the DA said no jury would ever convict him. There was no evidence. He would either blindfold me or wear a mask. I *never saw him*. Nobody ever saw him near the house," I said simply. "And the house isn't listed in his name. It belongs to one of his former administrative assistant—it was on the market, had been for a year. But strangely enough, nobody ever came out to view it. This woman, his former assistant, had been dating a man who I was supposedly having an affair with. A dozen people will claim they saw us flirting. I worked with him on a committee. That was it. But people would swear they'd seen us together. And Stefan…well, everybody believed *him*. Nobody believed me."

I felt drained and tired. I wanted to sleep, but I had to get this out.

"I hadn't seen him. There was no evidence. The DA said no jury would ever convict him." Staring at the wall now, I said, "He just got away with it. All of it."

Jenks' arms tightened around me and his voice was a low, ragged growl. "I want him dead."

"I just want him out of my life. Forever."

He took me to bed.

Fully clothed, the two of us stretched out on the massive sprawl of his king-sized bed and he didn't turn off the lights.

I lay down first, all but hugging the edge of the bed and Jenks stretched out next to me, on his side, facing me. "You going to stay there all night like that?"

I just stared at him.

He sighed. "Are you comfortable?"

"Um…"

Then he held out his hand.

I inched my way over to him.

Eventually I worked my way into his arms and pressed my face to his chest, breathing in the scent of him. I found myself tracing the lines of the tattoo that spread out down his right arm, visible under the sleeve of his shirt. "Why are you still here?" I asked him softly.

"I live here," he said reasonably. Then he pushed his hand into my hair, his fingers seeking out my scalp. My lids drooped as he started to massage. "Maybe you should close your eyes and get some rest, sugar."

"I don't mean that." Sleep sounded nice. "Why are you even around me? I'm a mess, Dillian. You can't tell me you haven't noticed that. I'm not remotely normal and I don't know if I'll ever even come close to being normal again. I have nightmares. I can't sleep without light. I have to drink one kind of water and I can't leave my apartment without checking the locks four times over. Sometimes even five or six or ten."

"There were worse things in the world, Shadow. I'm where I want to be."

I swallowed and then shifted back enough to look at him. The next part was going to be hard but I needed to say it. "I want to…"

That sounded lame. It sounded so lame. I was already with him, wasn't I?

"I wanted to…" Have sex? Fuck? Make love? Darting a look up at him, I saw a dark, hooded expression in his eyes and if I wasn't mistaken, there was hunger there. I reached up and touched his mouth. "I want you," I said, forcing the words out through my tight throat. "I want you more than I've ever wanted anything. But I don't know if I even can."

He startled me by rolling me onto my back, settling between my thighs, the solid, heavy weight of him tucked hard against me. His gaze held mine, confident and steady as he started to rock against me. Through the material of my skirt and the petticoat, I felt him, the thick heavy ridge of his cock and I could almost imagine him inside me.

"I think you can. And I bet, if you close your eyes right now and let yourself try, you'd think the same," he whispered, reaching up and stroking the rough pads of his fingers across my collarbone, left bare by the low-cut neck of my dress. "But…now isn't a good time. You're upset and you're not in a good place." He lowered his head, rubbed his lips across mine. "When it is a good time, you'll be ready. You'll want the same thing I do and that's to feel me come inside you so deep, you'll never want to be without me again."

I shuddered at the low, raw sound of his voice stroking over my skin like a velvet glove. And the look in his eyes was one of confidence and heat. Sliding my hand up his chest, I touched his jaw. "Are you so certain it will be that easy?"

"Yes." He turned his face into my hand and pressed a kiss against my palm, a hot, open-mouthed kiss that sent my pulse climbing up to a rhythm that just couldn't be healthy. And I didn't care.

Moments later, he rolled away and tucked me up against him. It had been a very long time since I'd had a man wrap himself around me in bed. The guys I'd been with in college had been more for doing the deed, then getting to sleep.

This was new.

I didn't know how to handle it.

I *liked* it—a lot.

But it was…weird.

"I'm here, I'm with you, because it's where I want to be, Shadow," Jenks said softly and I felt him smile against my brow. "You caught my eye almost from the first and then I kept seeing all these little things that just draw me in. You looked so shy and nervous every time I saw you, but then you forgot that sketchbook of yours and I saw all the dirty little pictures. I don't think there was enough cold water in the entire state to cool me down by the time I was done looking through that."

He surprised a laugh out of me and I poked him in the ribs. "Stop it," I mumbled as blood rushed up to stain my cheeks. Embarrassed, I kept my face tucked against his chest even when he continued to laugh, trying to get me to look at him.

"You have no idea how many times I wished I had just kept that damn thing." He pressed his lips to my ear. "I'm getting in a bad state right now, just thinking about it. You know which one I'm thinking about?"

I groaned. "Would you stop?"

His hand slid up my back, toyed with the ribbons that tied behind my neck. "Stop it? Are you nuts?" His voice was a hot, low murmur against my skin.

"You're probably are all hung up about that one at the end." I squirmed around and put my back against his chest. I was so hot, I couldn't breathe.

But I couldn't look at him either.

He laid his hand on my hair and stroked it up, then down. "No. There was one about halfway through. Of you. You're standing in front of a mirror, staring at yourself, and it's like you're trying to figure out what you see when you looking at your reflection." He cupped my left breast in his hand and pushed his thigh between mine. "I have this idea in my head, of me standing behind you, and you're naked, just like you were in that sketch. And I'll tell you what I see, so maybe you can rethink how you see yourself."

"I didn't want to see myself at all. I looked in the mirror and just saw the thing I'd been reduced to, in all those months when I was trapped. Then as time passed, I slowly started to see somebody else, but the woman

I saw wasn't strong. Just a broken, tired victim. I wanted to be more." Sighing, I closed my eyes. "I still want that. I just don't know how to get there."

"I want you to see what I see." He brushed my hair back and his thumb traced along the faint scar left over from surgery, all but hidden in my hairline. "I've seen this before, wondered what it was from. Now I know… and it makes it that much easier for me to tell you what I see." He touched his lips to the scar. "I see a survivor."

That sounds better than victim, I guess.

He caught one of my hands and lifted it to his lips. His tongue touched my palm and I gasped at the contact. "I see your hands and I think beautiful…think of all the beauty you make with them."

He lowered my hand to the bed and then brushed his lips against my shoulder. "I see these and I think strong. You carry too much."

Something that felt like tears pricked at my eyes. Turning my face into the pillow, I bit back the tears.

I didn't want to cry.

Not anymore.

He guided me around and when he cupped my face, his thumb stroked over my lip while he kissed my closed eyes. "I look at you now," he said softly. "And I see a woman who's tired. We should sleep."

Sleep.

Yeah.

I needed sleep.

But even as much as I needed it, I also feared it.

I feared the nightmares.

▲▼▲

A storm was breaking over the water when I woke.

I woke alone.

The scent of coffee teased me out of the bed and I padded out of the bedroom. The cottage had one of those open floor plans and from the doorway of the bedroom, I could see across the living room, clear into the kitchen. Jenks was standing at the stove, wearing nothing but a pair of low-slung workout pants.

The scents of bacon and coffee flooded the air and my belly growled.

Without turning around, he called out, "I've got a cup over here waiting for you."

I guess that meant I needed to join him.

Nerves chewed at me, gnawed at me.

I'd been nervous like this before, but only once.

Maybe even not quite like this. The one thing that might have compared had been my wedding night and although Stefan had been…proficient as a lover, he hadn't been overly proficient at giving a damn about me.

I'd had less *talented* lovers before him who had been…well, better lovers.

But I'd never been in a position like this. Maybe that was why I felt so much more anxious as I crossed over to stand in the kitchen, wearing the wrinkled dress I'd been so worried about yesterday, my hair a matted nightmare. Any attempt to look nice for him would be futile.

Jenks turned to look at me and the smile he gave me, that slow one that tugged up the corners of his mouth, lit up his face and it seemed as if he didn't care that I wasn't wearing perfectly applied makeup or that my dress looked like hell.

"Did you sleep?" he asked, taking the coffee from the counter and holding it out for me.

"Yeah. Better than I'd thought," I said, shrugging. I took a sip and sighed as the caffeine hit my system and started to sing. Plucking at my dress, I murmured, "I need to go home. Shower. Change."

"You can shower here. I can lend you a pair of shorts and a T-shirt."

I stared at his broad chest and then down at my body. "Nothing of yours would fit me."

"The shorts will be long on you, maybe a little snug in the hips, but they'll fit. You wouldn't have to wear the dress home."

I shrugged, about to dismiss the idea. But then I realized, if I wore his clothes home, maybe I could keep the shirt. I could sleep in it. Have his scent wrapped around me. It was foolish. It was silly. And the thought of sleeping in something that smelled of him filled my heart with something hot and twisty and soft. With a jerky nod, I moved to the table. "I might."

"Okay. Let me know after you eat."

Worrying my lower lip, I folded my hands in my lap and looked around. "Do you work today?" I'd never asked him, I realized, what he did.

His hands stilled, one gripping the skillet, the other holding the spatula. "Work?"

"Yeah. I don't even know what you do. You're at the beach a lot. Do you work somewhere around there?"

He shot me a look over his shoulder, an off-handed smile on his face. "I do software consulting for the most part."

"Software consulting?" I guess my surprise must have shown in my voice because he shot me an amused look.

"What were you expecting?"

"I don't know." I looked him up and down, then shook my head. "Something a little more…physical?"

"You were thinking I'm all brawn and no brain." He clicked his tongue then pointed the fork at me. "I'm half brain, half brawn, I'll have you know."

I went red in the face, feeling a little foolish. "So are you working today?"

"Nice thing about being a consultant…I can pick and choose my own hours. I'll put in a few later on." He glanced at me, his gaze lingering on my hands.

I realized I was still fussing with the dress.

I wanted out of it. I hadn't been wearing it all that long. It wasn't even nine. I'd put it on around six, but the thought of sleeping in it, not showering…it was making me twitchy and that was a feeling I knew all too well.

The more I thought about it, the more desperately I needed that shower, but he was almost done making breakfast and I couldn't just dive into the bathroom when he was being nice.

To distract myself, I moved over to the window and stared outside. "I don't know what software consulting is exactly, but you must make a killing. You've got an incredible view here." I lifted my hand and pressed it to the glass, sighing a little as I watched the waves crashing onto the sand. The leaden clouds, the rain pounding down outside made me feel as if we were alone in the world, just us in this little cottage. Oddly enough, if I had been in my house, I might have felt *too* isolated.

Here, with Jenks, it was perfect.

I wasn't being kept away from the world, my freedom stolen from me, and I wasn't here because I was too afraid to reach out.

I was in here because I wanted to be.

And he was with me because he wanted to be.

"You ready to eat?"

Startled, I looked up, saw his reflection in the glass, just behind me. "You're quieter than a cat."

"You're just lost in your thoughts." He brushed my hair aside and pressed his lips to my neck. "Hungry?"

I shivered at the feel of his lips on my skin.

"Yes."

CHAPTER TEN

"Here you go."

Dillian put a T-shirt and a pair of workout pants down on the long expanse of countertop by the sink, meeting my eyes in the mirror. "Anything else you need?"

My heart thudded in my throat.

I'd found a toothbrush still in the package in the closet and I'd swiped it, used it to brush my teeth.

I'd washed my face, combed my hair so I didn't look like a complete zombie.

I hadn't lied when I told him I was hungry.

But I was hungry for more than food. I was hungry for sensation, for touch, for words, for the feel of skin against mine, to feel a hard body moving on my own and to have a pair of eyes watching me as I stared up at a man who actually wanted to be with me.

Yes, I needed something.

And I thought maybe Jenks might be the one person who could give it to me. He was the only one I'd met in the past couple of years, that was certain. I'd noticed other men, but I'd never felt like this and despite the nerves shaking and quivering in my body, I was determined that I would at least try.

He'd said last night was a bad time.

It wasn't last night now.

Licking my lips, I turned around and reached out, spread my hand out over his heart.

His gaze, heavy-lidded and hooded, came up to meet mine.

"I think I need you."

The words came out steadier than I would have thought possible, although my voice was all but gone. My blood roared in my ears and my heart beat so hard I could barely breathe. But I said the words, and more, he heard them. His hand closed around my wrist, his thumb stroking over my pulse. Slowly, he guided my hand down, holding it at my side as he moved in until I was trapped between him and the counter, his body a hot brand against mine. "I thought we said this wasn't a good time." He spoke softly.

"We said last night wasn't. Or rather you did. I agreed, then. Now I'm thinking it is." Slowly, his fingers uncurled from my wrist and I surprised us both when I reached up and pressed my hand to the starburst tattoo on his chest. Under my hand, his heart slammed hard against my palm and my own echoed, a ragged, desperate beat that left me shaky and lightheaded.

He slid one hand up my arm. "You still want that shower?"

My head felt unbalanced as I nodded. "Maybe you could…"

"I wouldn't mind seeing you all wet and naked, sugar." He tugged on the tie until it came free, seeking out the hidden zipper at my side and giving it a tug. It took him less than two minutes to have me naked in front of him and then I stood there, trembling and nervous, while he cupped my waist in his hands and stared at me.

"Fuck…" he breathed out and then he went to his knees.

I blinked and then I cried out as he leaned in, caught one nipple in his mouth.

Sensation, a storm of it, slammed into me. His mouth, hot and wet, his arm around my waist, strong and solid, while his free hand gripped my hip as though he thought I might pull away. His teeth tugged lightly against my flesh, just enough that I felt the edge and it was almost more pleasure than I could stand. My knees tried to give out and he guided me back so that the sink supported me.

I started to push my hands into his hair, desperate for more, desperate for everything, but before I could, he caught my wrists and surged upward, burying his face against my neck. "Stop…gotta stop or I'll be sinking my dick into you right here and we both should have more than that, but I'll damn well make sure *you* have more," he muttered.

"Jenks?"

"Shower." He turned around and strode to the shower, tucked behind a simple frosted-glass wall and turned it on. As steam started to billow out, he came back to me and led me over to it. For a minute, I lingered, missing his warmth and the feel of his hands on me.

His gaze caught mine. Then he dipped his head and rubbed his lips against mine. The lightest of kisses. "I'll be there in a second," he promised.

So I went in. The hot water slid like silk over me and I closed my eyes, tried to calm my breathing, tried to calm myself. There wasn't much of that happening and I braced one hand against the wall. Was I going to do this? Hell, yes. Could I actually *get* through it? That was the trickier question.

Water splashed behind me and that was all the warning I had before his arms came around me.

A gasp hitched in my throat as his body aligned with mine. All that glorious, golden skin, naked against mine. For a long, aching moment, I just let myself feel.

It's possible to feel *too* much. Even if it felt good. Just like you could go too long feeling *nothing*…sensory deprivation is a painful thing and that was why I clung to every last bit of sensory pleasure I could get now. I wrapped myself in it, steeped myself in it.

But there wasn't enough of this. The hard, solid strength of his arm around me, his muscled chest sliding against my back, the soft scrape of stubble against my neck as he brushed my wet hair out of the way and kissed my shoulder.

"You're wet…naked. Just like a mermaid now," he whispered. One hand smoothed down my thigh and I trembled as it stroked back upward, just a few scant inches from my core.

Steam wrapped around us as he reached over. From the corner of my eye, I saw the built-in dispenser and then I caught the subtle, sexy scent that seemed to cling to him. That soap, whatever it was, men of the world needed to invest it. It would all but seduce women from the scent alone. Moments later, he had the suds clinging to me as he washed me from head to toe, including my hair. "Close your eyes," he said, nudging me under the dual shower heads.

I felt water pounding down on me from multiple angles and then he drew me back out. I watched as he washed himself and my breathing sped up. Maybe now. Would we go to bed now? Or would he—

My heart slammed so hard against my ribs, I wouldn't be surprised if it was bruised. He'd reached up, pulled one of the shower heads down. Now, as he crowded up against me, he leaned in. "Close your eyes."

Breathing seemed almost impossible. "Why?"

"Because I'm going to make you feel," he said.

He couldn't have said anything that would have gotten me to listen any faster.

I couldn't relax, though. Eyes closed, my breathing ragged, I stood there, rigid even when he nudged me back against the wall.

And then I felt the water. It was a pulsating rain against my thigh and I jolted in shock, my eyes flying open. He was watching me. "Let me, Shadow," he said, his voice dark and raw. "You want to feel...I'll make you feel."

How could I say no to that?

His free hand caught one of my knees, guiding it up, exposing me and then he started to tease me, that jet of water going up, then down, each time coming closer and closer to the heart of me.

When he finally turned it to me, I almost collapsed at the sheer sensation. I was already wet, already aching. The blast of heat and pressure from the water was a thrill against my senses and it left me reeling, threatened to send me flying and I thought I might die from it. I reached out, grasping for him, my fingers sinking into the thick pad of muscles atop his shoulders.

"Just let go," he murmured, his voice steady, gentle, almost soothing. Even as the water tormented and teased. "Feel it...let go."

I sobbed, the strength draining out of me and then he shifted me around, sliding on down and I cried out as he traced my entrance. "Come for me now."

I did. I couldn't stop it and I didn't want to.

▲▼▲

My legs were almost too weak, but I managed to move out of the shower. Clutching the towel he'd wrapped around me, I looked around, dazed, trying to drag my thoughts back on track, but I didn't even have a chance for that.

I saw him in the mirror and looked up.

Our gazes locked and then he moved, spinning me around and boosting me up onto the sink.

"Last chance," he muttered against my mouth.

"For what?"

"To tell me to wait. That you need more time. I'll back off if you need me to." He gripped my head between his hands and the look in his eyes was one of torment. "Fuck, Shadow. Tell me you don't need me to."

"I don't *want* you to," I said and then I reached for him.

He hauled me against him and then we were moving.

The bed was a soft, welcome relief and I cried out as I felt him between my thighs, the folds of my sex slick and wet, the ache inside me spreading. He paused and shoved up, and I glared at him but all he did was scramble for something by the bed.

I heard something tear and then I saw the glint of foil.

Condoms. He had condoms.

He tore one open and I watched as he levered up onto his knees. My throat went dry as I watched him put on the condom. Something that might have been fear started to whisper inside me as I stared at him.

So clearly, I could remember the last time a man had touched me, been inside me—it had been nothing like this, but it didn't matter. Those memories, once imprinted on the mind, the flesh, the heart, the soul, they never fully fade and now they came clawing to the surface.

A hand touched my face, fingers spread wide over my jaw, the tips spearing into my hair with his thumb pressed up under my jaw to angle my head back. "Stop," Jenks ordered, his voice low and harsh, the intensity in it all but throbbing. "I see where your mind is going…don't let him come here."

Wrapping my hand around his wrist, I stared at him. "I don't know if I can stop it. What if I freak out?"

"Then you do…and we try again." He came down over me and the shock of his body against mine, the pleasure of it was one that left me all but ready to melt into him. "But don't bring him here. He's taken enough from you. Don't give him this."

Was it that simple?

I knew it wasn't.

He probably did, too. But I could do everything in my power to shove Stefan out of my head. If I focused more on Jenks…I skimmed my hand along his arm, let my fingers play along the hard curve of muscle, felt them jump under my touch.

"I don't want him here." I stared into his eyes.

He pressed a kiss to my cheek, my nose, my mouth. "He isn't here. It's just us."

His cock was a heavy brand against my belly, sheathed in the condom and slick with the lubricant. Closing my eyes, I gave a tiny shove against his chest and he went up, his weight balanced on his elbows. As he hovered against me, I continued to watch only his eyes, learning him with my hands. Everywhere I touched, he was hard muscle and smooth skin and heat.

I could feel the need pulsing inside him, but he didn't rush me. The driving hunger that had pushed me up until just a few minutes ago was gone and caution led me now. I had to…I don't know what I had to do. There was more than curiosity in this, more than caution. It was as though I needed to learn more about him and learning more about him taught me something about myself.

We ended up with him sprawled on his back and me kneeling beside him, my face almost painfully red as I stroked my hands across him. I'd touched almost every blessed inch of him, except where I needed to touch him the most.

A pained sound left him as I dragged my nails across his thigh and I looked up, saw his head arched back, the veins standing out as he groaned out my name. "Did I…" I stopped myself from asking. The answer scared me. Desire was a monster inside me and I ached for more than I could describe, but if he said something—

"You're driving me crazy. Don't stop," he muttered, grasping his cock in one hand.

Mesmerized, I stared, watching as he fisted himself, dragged his hand up, then down. Under the thin shield of the latex, the fat, round head of his cock was swollen and my mouth watered. I wanted to…

"Stop."

I shot him a look, startled.

He grasped his balls in his other hand and a vicious spasm of want wrenched at me as he stroked himself, harder and faster. And all the while he watched me. All but daring me. "Stop looking at me like that, like you're all but dying to put your mouth on me," he said. "If you won't do it, then just…"

My mouth fell open.

And that long, powerful body shuddered. "Fuck, Shadow. You're killing me."

My mouth.

On him.

Maybe if I just did it—

I didn't let myself think.

His voice was a ragged snarl that echoed around us as I leaned down and did exactly what we both seemed to need. I hated that the rubber was there, even though part me understood it. Smart sex, blah, blah, blah. Who cared about smart?

The rest of me was too caught up in everything else. The way he was shuddering against me. The way one of his hands cupped my cheek— softly, gently, almost as if he couldn't believe I was doing this.

I couldn't either.

His body arched up, rocking to me as I moved down on him, taking as much of his cock as I could, half-choking as he hit the back of my throat, and then moving back. It was awkward. I'd never been very good at this, a fact that—

My brain shut that thought down before I could finish. I hadn't been very good at it, but I could learn. Jenks liked it when I paused at the top and scraped my teeth against him and I'd seen how he'd grasped his sac in his hand so I did the same thing.

That made his breathing came faster and the muscles in his thighs bunched hard and tight.

I liked that.

But then, just as he started to rock harder and faster against me and my head was spinning with the delight of all of this, he stopped. Seconds later, I was on my back, staring up at the ceiling and then shoving up onto my elbows to look down at him.

He knelt between my thighs and I could see the top of his head as he caught my hips in his hands. "My turn. You're going to drive me crazy," he muttered. "You…fuck. Shadow, just let me…"

Let him?

A shaky moan escaped me as he pressed his mouth against me.

I had to stare at him, because if I closed my eyes for even a second, I was going to go back to dark and ugly places, but it wasn't a hard thing to see him kneeling between my thighs, his body so dark against my own, the top edges of the snarling wolf visible as he moved against me.

Need throbbed, vibrating inside. I had to choke back a scream as he stabbed his tongue against me. My clit pulsed and that pleasure was almost too brutal, almost too much. He growled against me and slid me a look, his gaze practically glowing. "Scream for me. I want to hear you come. I want you to break and sigh and fall apart. I'll catch you, Shadow. I swear."

It was an intimate sort of promise, one I wanted to trust.

Then he slid two fingers inside me and I had no choice. The climax slammed into me and I broke. I didn't sigh—I sobbed out his name, and I flew so high, reaching for his shoulders and clutching at him, needing something to keep me from flying into a thousand pieces.

And then, as he pressed a soft kiss to my inner thigh, I started to fall.

He was there to catch me. Nothing had ever felt so right.

His eyes dark and hungry, he settled between my thighs.

"It's just us," he murmured.

I nodded, the motion awkward and jerky, my breath a sob in my throat as I wrapped my arms around him.

Just us.

The blunt head probing between my thighs was thick, thicker than I was used to and my breath hitched in my throat as he started to stretch me. Everything in the world narrowed down, focused down to nothing but this...the way it felt as he slowly filled me. His gaze caught mine as he withdrew and I caught my breath when he sank back inside, a little deeper, and he pulsed, throbbed inside me. I could feel it.

I clenched around him, unable to stop it. The thick, long ridge of his cock jerked in response and I whimpered, drawing up one knee. A gasp lodged in my throat and I squirmed on the bed, thrashing and straining to get closer.

A slow smile twisted his lips and it sent a surge of embarrassment twisting through me even as the delight burned me from the inside out. I tried to look away but he tangled a hand in my hair and muttered, "No."

It is too intimate, I thought. Far too intimate, but he wouldn't let me look away, wouldn't let me escape that moment. "It's us," he said against my mouth. "You're here with me."

"With you." The words came out of me in a gasp as he surged deep, so deep, and then he withdrew and as I watched him, he did it again, and again. I could feel myself tighten around him, felt an answering pulse deep within me. Digging my nails into his shoulders, I arched up, working myself against him as the sensation spread through me.

Sensation—*that* was something I could get lost in. The heat of his body against mine. The glide of sweat-slickened flesh. The way his hand slid down my hip and caught my butt, canted me higher as he sank into me, deeper this time, almost all the way in.

And then he was all the way in. I could feel him, his cock gloved inside me, his belly to mine, his heart to mine...and maybe it could even go deeper than that.

His hand came back to my face, cupped it. His thumb swept across my lower lip. "You with me?"

"Yes." I nodded as I said it, the word stuttering out of me and I knew there was absolutely no place else I wanted to be in that moment.

He said nothing more. His body rocked against mine and I felt the rhythm, the heat and the beauty of it. Jenks seemed to notice every little thing—if my breath hitched when he stroked the underside of my breast, he'd devote insane amounts of time doing just that. When he shifted against me and I felt the pressure against my clitoris, he noticed and then a supernova exploded inside me as he angled his body so that every stroke had him riding me just there.

And his voice… He never stopped talking. While I gasped for air, when sometimes the pleasure all but blinded me, he talked.

"Just like that…no, don't close your eyes, I want to see you when I make you come, Shadow…"

"Kiss me. Open your mouth…"

"Shadow, wrap your legs around me…"

It was as if he wanted me to remember who was inside me.

I wanted to think I couldn't forget. But sometimes, the monsters will steal inside your head.

They didn't. Not then.

And when I couldn't handle any more, he caught my hand, tangled our fingers and I felt his control shatter, just as he'd shattered me so many times. That beautiful body that I'd drawn time after time now arched over me, a powerful, taut bow. He came against me, hard and deep, and once more, I climaxed. This time, I wasn't alone.

CHAPTER ELEVEN

The monster found me later that day.

Jenks insisted on coming home with me and I was so glad he did.

If I had gone inside and found the destruction on my own, I think I might still be sitting in a curled up, terrified little ball, outside on my porch.

Instead, I was sitting on the couch in my neighbor's place—I'd never even met him before today. To my surprise, I was more composed than I would have thought I could be.

Sooner or later, I *would* fall apart.

As long as it didn't happen while I was talking to the cops. As long as it waited until I was alone.

"…glad you weren't in there alone."

Startled, I looked up, met my neighbor's eyes. Jones. His name was Jones. That was his first name. Jones Alan Brown. Odd name. Kind eyes, with a lot of laugh lines. "I'm sorry," I said, forcing myself to smile. "My mind was wandering."

"Understandable." He nodded and looked back through his door. We could see inside to where the cops were looking around. Jenks was at the door, his hands on his hips, a look on his face that would have had me backing away if I didn't know him. "I was saying, it's a good thing you weren't there alone last night."

Little black dots started to crowd in on my vision at those words. *Alone… If I'd been alone…*

Some part of me realized that Stefan wouldn't have done anything that would have attracted attention toward him. Not after the little interlude at the restaurant. The waitress had taken too much notice of him. She hadn't liked him. He wouldn't do anything until that incident faded from her memory. Oh, he was behind the destruction of my home but it wouldn't be traced back to him.

He wouldn't do anything directly to me, though.

Not yet.

"Do you have any idea who might have done it?" Jones asked, still staring at my front door.

Automatically, I started to lie. To deny.

That is what a victim does. We brush it aside. We explain away those little bruises, laugh off how clumsy we are.

My mouth had gone dry.

Jenks slid his gaze my way.

I felt the burning intensity of it and the truth came tearing out of me. "My ex-husband."

Those words hung there, ugly and raw, like acid on a wound and the pain of it spread.

Slowly, Jones turned his head and looked at me.

"Your ex."

I nodded. Prepared myself to see him back away. Nobody wanted to get involved in ugly little things like that. Not many people had *seen* Stefan's true face, but there had been a few. A very, very few. And almost every single one had distanced themselves from it.

Jones reached over and covered my hands with his.

"How bad was it?"

A shaky sigh escaped me. "Bad. Very bad."

His eyes studied me. Then he nodded. "I'm sorry."

"Me, too." With a watery laugh, I pulled my hands away and rose from the couch, pacing the room, unable to stay still. It was hard to be still, hard to sit there and watch as the cops continue to go through my house. I could see them pass back and forth in front of the door occasionally. All of this brought those hidden wounds out of me and I felt exposed all over again.

Unable to stay still a moment longer, I practically tore out of there and went to stand just inside my doorway. Tremors shook me as Jenks' gaze cut my way.

He came to stand in front of me. One hand, big and rough, came up, cradling my cheek. Fury tightened his features, but his voice was level as he asked, "You okay?"

I was surprised at my answer. "Oh, I'm just peachy. Thought maybe I'd go for a Sunday stroll."

A slow smile curled his lips and he moved in, hooking an arm around my neck. "I can think of a good destination," he murmured, his lips against my ear. "I want to find that chickenshit ex of yours and beat him bloody."

Any response I might have had would have to wait.

"Ms. Harper?"

The sound of my name had me pulling back from Jenks and turning. It was Detective Barry.

When I'd moved here, after days of hiding out, I'd finally convinced myself I needed to tell a cop about my ex. I needed to tell a cop about the fact that I had men watching me.

I'd eventually gone to Detective Barry.

I'd heard about her from a local women's shelter. I'd donated money and some clothes there, and sometimes, I'd go in and talk to the woman in charge. She was the one who'd recommended Barry.

I was glad I'd found her.

Occassionally, she'd send me an email.

Sometimes, she would just stop by.

But that wasn't the case today. She had been keeping an eye on me, just as she'd promised.

Detective Barry had been the one who step in when Stefan had tried to mess things up for Seth and she'd been the one who handled the calls about the men who watched me. I wasn't surprised to see her now.

She looked to be in her thirties, but her black hair was already going silver at her temples and her eyes were wise beyond her years. Her skin was a deep, smooth brown and when she smiled—which wasn't often—it changed her entire face.

Right now, she wasn't smiling.

She looked at my open door, at me, at Jenks.

"Detective."

Without waiting for an invitation, she came inside. "I heard you had some trouble."

"Yes." Jenks' fingers tightened around my hand and I glanced down. When had I taken his hand? Had he taken mine? I didn't know. But it felt good to have somebody there with me. To have *him* there with me. Looking back at the detective, I forced a smile. It didn't last long, but I didn't have to waste time on pleasantries or niceties, not with her. It was why I had liked her. "I was going to call you. I kept thinking about it and then I'd start to and another thought would enter my mind…" I stopped, heaving out a sigh. "I can't concentrate today."

Understanding shone in her eyes. "I'd say you've got enough in your head." Then she shrugged and turned to stare into my apartment. "You know I have your name flagged. I heard about this. That's why I'm here."

Numb, I nodded.

She put a hand on my shoulder, squeezed. "You're holding up pretty well."

Was I? I felt like I was going to fall apart, right at the seams.

She studied my face for another moment and then shifted her attention to Jenks. He met her gaze straight on. I wondered how she saw him, how he saw her. I remembered how I first saw him—so sexy, larger than life and nothing I could ever reach out and touch.

His thumb rubbed across the sensitive skin of my wrist and I thought about that morning. Last night. The night on the beach.

I'd done so much more than reach out and touch.

Most of the reaching out had been on his part, but I hadn't taken off running, either. That had to count for something.

And no matter what had happened to my home, I felt like I'd taken another little piece of myself back. One of those pieces that had been ripped out and left to wither and die inside that tight, dark, dank little basement.

"Detective Louise Barry."

Pulled out of my reverie, I watched as Jenks nodded at the cop. He didn't offer to shake her hand, didn't offer his name until she asked.

"Got anything other than Jenks?" she asked, lifting a brow at him.

"I do." Then he shrugged and glanced over at the apartment. "I already gave all my info to the officers. I was kind of thinking about taking Shadow to the coffee shop, trying to get her to get something to eat. Neither of us have had anything since breakfast and I know she won't eat unless food is actually put in front of her. It will be a while before she can get into the kitchen, I figure."

Eat?

I didn't want to eat.

Except I knew how bad it was to go without food and thinking about it made that desperate, terrible feeling return. It was an echo of the way I'd felt in those final days before I'd escaped hell. When I realized that maybe, just maybe, Stefan was done tormenting me. That he'd let me starve down there. Trapped, helpless, alone.

No, I wasn't hungry. But I'd make myself eat.

"The police will need to talk to you." Barry eyed us narrowly.

"I know that," I said sourly, cutting Jenks off before he could say anything. But they weren't even close to done. I could see that. "The coffee shop is fifteen minutes away and it will take maybe fifteen minutes to get a sandwich this time of day. We'll be back in under an hour. Maybe then they'll be done and my head will clear enough that I can actually think when I talk to them."

She opened her mouth to say something else, an objection, an argument. I could see it in her eyes. Just as I could see whatever agreement or conciliation that Jenks was going to offer. He was playing my protector. He did it a lot and a huge part of me was grateful. I didn't mind at all and there were no alarm bells about how he did it. I'd heard alarm bells before, and I'd silenced them.

This was just him, trying to shield me.

But while I didn't hear alarm bells, I was tired of being shielded, tired of being afraid. Tired of just about everything.

Lifting a hand, I pushed between them and started to walk to the door. "Detective, if I don't get out of here for a few minutes, I'm not going to be any good to them. To you. To myself. I need to breathe and I need to think."

And while I had no desire to eat, I'd damn well make myself do it.

The trip to the coffee shop hadn't taken long enough. We were already back at my house, sitting on the front step. With a sandwich on my lap, I tried to summon up the interest in eating it, but I just couldn't.

I looked down at Jenks. He had his hips against the porch's wrought iron railing, his gaze roaming all around, seeming to rest on nothing, but I knew he was taking in everything.

Including my lack of appetite. I held up a bit of bacon. "I am eating. A little." Popping the rest of it in my mouth, I shrugged. "Just not very hungry."

"Because you're worried about your ex." His gaze focused on me.

My fingers tightened on the sandwich and the bread, still soft from the oven, crumpled. Carefully, I put it down and reached for the napkin I'd laid across my lap. "Jenks—" I paused and then said, "Dillian, you can't understand what it's like. If I wasn't eating because I was *worried*, then I'd just never eat." Sliding a look across the street, I saw the curtains drop as the skinny, dark-haired man lost himself to the darkness of his room. One of my shadows—the one Jenks had scared within an inch of his life. The one who watched me most days. He was the one who disappeared four hours a week and allowed me the freedom to go to the beach. But he no longer followed me when I left the house.

That was something.

Rubbing my mouth with my fingertips, I watched those dingy, faded curtains and decided it was time to stop ignoring it. I could have that man's name. I could know who he was and what had made it so easy for Stefan to make him agree to this.

It settled something inside me. There was a time to hide. Deep inside, I knew that. To survive, sometimes you had to hide. To survive, you had to tuck your head, protect it as blows rained down around you. To survive, you had to lie there and try hard not to cry as a hand squeezed your throat while the man who'd promised to love you tore your body and crushed your soul. To survive, you had to sit in the corner and smell your own filth and conserve water and wait and hope.

Sooner or later, though, if you stayed in hiding, you started to die inside.

I had hidden long enough and those pieces of me that I had tried so hard to take back were shriveling away.

Looking down at the crushed remains of my sandwich, I peeled the bread away and found the other piece of bacon. I wasn't hungry, but I made myself eat. "You can't know what it's like," I said again, staring at the pavement. "The fear is always a part of me. It's in my blood, in my skin, in my bones. He put it there when he broke me, when he beat me, when he broke those bones, when he bruised my skin, when he made me bleed."

I lapsed into silence and forced myself to eat more, picking through the sandwich. The more I ate, the hungrier I realized I was and finally, I'd managed to eat the ham, most of the turkey I hadn't shredded, and every one of the tomatoes and all of the cheese.

"What are you going to do?" Jenks asked when I finally forced myself to look up.

"Do?"

His only response was a short, terse nod.

I shrugged. "I'm not sure yet what I *can* do. He's not so stupid that he would leave anything that would connect him to this. I'll file the report. Give them his name, but…"

"Are you leaving?" He cut me off, coming to kneel in front of me, his hands cupping up to bracket my skull, forcing me to look at him.

The question caught me off guard.

"Leaving?" I stared at him, confused. Why would I leave? This was home. The only home I'd known since my parents had died. It had been more than a decade since I'd felt like I even *had* a home.

"Yeah. Are you going to take off now that he's shown up here?"

Slowly, I reached up, curling my hands around his wrists. I needed that connection. It seemed that I needed every connection I could get with Jenks. Every one I could get, and it still wasn't enough. Stroking my thumbs along his skin, I leaned in and pressed my brow to his.

"He's known where I was since I got here. Why would I leave a place where I have friends? A place where I'm happy?"

He rubbed his nose against mine, then kissed me—a gentle kiss, his mouth just barely grazing mine. "Are you happy? You don't seem to be happy...always looking over your shoulder, checking your locks. A few hours spent at the beach a few times a week and you spend that time huddled over your sketchbooks. That's not really being *happy*, Shadow."

"It is for me." I let go of his wrist, reached up and touched his jaw, felt the scrape of stubble against my palm. "You should have seen me the first few months, even the first year when I got away. I couldn't stand to leave for anything except college and I was like a church mouse, jumping at every little sound. It's probably a borderline miracle I'm able to leave home at all."

Turning his face into my palm, he kissed it, his tongue slipping out to tease my skin.

It was amazing what such a simple little touch could do.

"It's not that much of a miracle. You stopped letting him control you when you left the basement. And you started fighting when you tried to leave." He pulled back, watching me.

And I saw secrets glinting in his eyes.

"You were done letting him control you. The miracle is that you survived it."

Then his mouth caught mine and this kiss was such a wondering, gentle thing. It was like a hello, like a discovery, like a taste and a tease and so many other things I can't describe. His tongue twined with mine as his hands held me steady and it didn't matter that we were on the front step in broad daylight. It didn't matter that there were people around us and I was vaguely aware of a catcall coming from somewhere.

None of it mattered.

Nothing mattered except the way his fingers pushed into my hair to cradle the back of my head, the way the fingers of the other hand sought out the faded scars near my hairline to brush along those lines before stroking down my neck, my shoulder, my arm. He caught my hand in his and then finally lifted his head.

Emotion crashed inside me and I wanted to sigh, wanted to sob as I tucked my head into his shoulder. There was no way to describe how it felt, pressed against him, right there. Safe. Wanted. Needed. His hand smoothed down my back, rested on my hip.

"A huge part of me wants to tell you that you *should* leave."

I shivered at the words. It made something horrible and awful spread inside me. No…I wasn't going to be controlled. Even as something inside me twisted and died at the thought of pulling away, I made myself do that, rising on the step and staring down at him.

There was a strange little smile on his face.

I curled my hand into a fist as a tight, hot little ball gathered inside my chest.

Fury. It was *fury*.

"You don't get to tell me what to do, Dillian," I said softly.

I started to turn away.

His hand shot out, tangling in the material of my skirt. "I guess I wasn't clear in how I said that."

I glared down at him, reaching out to jerk my skirt away.

He let go, but it was to shift his grip to my ankle instead and that touch was emotionally and physically devastating. His thumb stroked along my skin, sent heat waves pulsing through me. This was one of those times when I damned how very much my body still craved, cried out for, any sort of physical stimuli.

"I said a part of me *wants* to tell you that," he said, his gaze locking on mine. That velvety brown pulsed hot, burned so intently. "You see, I know that's the last thing you can do. You need this place. You need what's yours. You need the home you've made and you need to find everything else that you're still missing inside. All the things he stole from you. I get that. I won't claim to understand all that you're looking for, but I know you need it."

The part of me that had been wilting started to warm again. Muscles that had locked tight went lax and I might have collapsed except I had a mad urge not to let him see just how much those words affected me. Just how *he* was starting to affect me. Trying to be casual about it, I tugged my ankle out of his grip and moved over to the opposite side of the porch, leaning against the railing and staring down the quiet street.

"I'm not leaving this place," I said, shaking my head. This was home. Maybe if I hadn't left it, I'd have become the woman I'd been on my way to becoming before Stefan had found me. I'd never know, but I definitely wasn't walking away from here again.

The rustic charm of the exposed brick walls, the wide-open design of my house, the huge windows that let in all the light. The way the windows faced out over the ocean and the sparkle of the sunlight reflecting off the water. It was an older home, but nothing about it spoke of old world elegance—it was all shabby chic and I loved it.

When I'd been married to Stefan, his home had looked like something from a high-fashion magazine—polished chrome, smooth lines, high gloss and endless expanses of black, broken up here and there with bursts of brilliant peacock blue or blood red. Very fashionable, very cutting edge. Very cold.

My home was warm, welcoming…and mine.

The door opened and I saw the officer standing there with Detective Barry, who glanced from me to Jenks and then gestured to the door. "We need to get to those questions," she said.

I nodded and looked at Jenks.

That smile of his, slow and steady, waited for me. "I'll be right here."

CHAPTER TWELVE

The police were finally gone. They'd left the door unlocked and although it left my spine crawling, I hadn't gotten up to lock it. Jenks was still outside and I couldn't work up the energy to go get him, or even move from the spot where I had stopped after the cops had left.

Numb, I sank to the floor, my skirt puddling around me as I reached for one of the sketchbooks.

It was one of the early ones. I knew each one and this one wouldn't have held anything too terribly risqué.

He'd destroyed them all, though.

Taken a knife to them, it looked like.

I sat there, so despondent, I didn't even jump when I heard the knock at the door.

"Yes?"

"It's me." Jenks' voice carried through the door and I sighed, touching the image of a woman's face. She'd been at the beach, nursing a baby. I'd drawn her, the way she had the blanket over her, covering them both, the little girl's feet poking out, her hand curled around her mother's finger. And he'd destroyed that one, too.

Every single one.

I'd had three books with me—the three I always took when I was out of the house because I never knew when I'd see something I had to draw, but those were all I had.

"Come on in," I said, my voice a ghost of itself.

Jenks heard me anyway.

The familiar sound of the locks sliding into place filled the room and my throat burned as he said, "The locks are set. Should I check them again?"

"No." I shook my head. It wouldn't do any good. I had to check them or it didn't count.

And just then, I couldn't make myself move.

His footsteps came my way but I still couldn't tear my eyes off the ruined image in front of me.

Minutes ticked by and then finally Jenks reached out and I didn't fight him as he took the portrait. Sometimes I wondered if I shouldn't give the images I drew to the people who'd inspired them. Not *all* of them, of course. If I saw a couple making out on the beach, I'd just as soon keep that private, but something like this, I'd rather that mom have it than to see it ruined.

"He destroyed all of them," I said, my voice ragged, my heart raw. My very soul felt crushed.

Jenks sat down behind me and curved his body behind mine. "The cops going to talk to him?"

Closing my eyes, I braced one elbow on my knee. "I gave them his name. The officers made the standard noises, but if I know Detective Barry, she'll poke around. But I know him. He wouldn't have been seen. *If* he was here at all. Chances are he paid somebody to come out here and do this…"

I stopped, paused.

"How did he get in?" I whispered, starting to shake. My skull felt like it was going to split apart.

He shouldn't have been able to get inside. It shouldn't have happened.

I had a good security system. It wouldn't keep people out of Fort Knox, but it damn well should have done its job here. Clambering to my feet, I practically ran to the table where I had put my purse. I grabbed my phone out, scrolled through the emails and my knees just about melted when I saw that not only had I not gotten alerts about the system being disarmed *today*, I hadn't gotten any last night. Not a one since I'd set the system yesterday.

Somehow, he'd figured out how to hack my system.

My work computer was set up in the little area between the living room and the kitchen. It had been intended to be a breakfast bar, but that served no purpose for me and worked a lot better as a work area. I was very, very glad it was close just then because if it had been more than four or five feet, my legs might have given out beneath me. As it was, I practically collapsed as I dropped down onto the seat.

The Mac took forever to load. Or so it seemed. It was a powerful beast, but just then, even a few seconds was a lifetime and it took too long for me to log into the website for the security system.

My password didn't work.

I tried to reset it, panicking when the site claimed the email didn't match.

Okay.

Okay.

"Shadow?"

I jumped when he stroked his hand down my hair. Immediately, that light touch was gone and he moved into my line of sight, staring at me, the look on his face the same one he might have given a feral cat. It didn't help my peace of mind any.

"I can't get into the website I use for my security system."

The few lines around his eyes tightened, the only sign he gave that he'd even heard me. After a beat or two, he shifted his chair around and studied the website. "What's going on?"

"I have a security system." I licked my lips and then gestured around the apartment. "There are...um, hidden cameras. It's overkill, it's para-noid and I know that, but I needed it. To feel safe."

"Why do you need that to feel safe?"

"I..." I licked my lips, tucking my hands into my lap as I tried to find the way to explain that wouldn't make me seem crazy. Crazier. "The weeks after I left him, I stayed in an apartment. When I was in the hospital, they put me in touch with a shelter for battered women and they worked me through what I needed to do to leave him. How to stay safe. It's never as easy as they say and they warned me it wouldn't be. But I had to try. I was in a nice, safe apartment. It had security guards. You couldn't get inside unless you had a key to the main gate. But he would get in."

Jenks brushed my hair back from my face, kept his hand curved around the back of my neck. "How do you know?"

"He used to make me do crazy shit when we were married. We had a housekeeper, a cook, but he was weird about who touched his personal things. That was my job, as his wife. He *instructed* me on things like fold-ing his underwear. Aligning his socks. Ordering things by color. Once I was away from him, it was..." I stopped, blowing out a breath as I tried to find the words. "Habit. It was habit, something engrained inside me and I kept doing it for almost six weeks after I left him, while I struggled to get the divorce finalized. He fought it all, every step of the way. And the police were no help. There was no evidence, just me all black and blue. One night, after the detective in charge of my case told me they didn't think they'd be able to prosecute, I broke down and threw everything in the cabinets out on the floor. All of my socks. All of my underwear. I was like a two-year-old having a tantrum."

It had been one of the more freeing events of my life. The next morning, I decided I was leaving.

Maybe they couldn't find the evidence they needed to prosecute and that wasn't a bad thing. That meant nothing held me in Boston. So I left the apartment.

I explained all of that and then had to stop, catching my breath as that fear gathered inside me again. Fear. Terror. *Rage*. "I went back, felt like I was finally taking control again, and I walked inside, prepared to see that mess. I didn't care. The food, I could throw out, or donate what wasn't ruined. My clothes, I could just pack. But everything was had been picked up. The house was neat as pin."

Nothing could describe that fear.

How it felt when I ran through the apartment, jerked open the drawers and saw the way my panties were *folded* and organized by style and color. All the briefs—I wore a lot of them in those days—in one neat area, while the bikinis were in another and everything was done in a pretty little rainbow of color.

The socks were the same, and the clothes in my closet had been organized in sections of summer and winter, casual and dress, bright color and drab.

"I was a fucking mess by the time the cops got there and they thought I'd lost my mind."

"Did they *question* him?"

My laugh held no humor. "Of course." My hands shook as I pushed my hair back from my face and the sensory memory, the feel of it on my neck, touching my skin, was more than I could handle. I clambered up from the bar, my limbs feeling too loose, my joints too tight as I headed down the hall to my bathroom. It was a disaster. The drawers had been upended, the precious little makeup I owned dumped out on the floor. One small basket remained on the shelf over my toilet. It figured that he wouldn't touch that—it held tampons a neat little case where I liked to keep them and a few pads. There was also a hair clip on the side of the shelf and I grabbed it, gathering my hair up and securing it, using the clip to hold it tightly.

"I gave them his name, and they went and spoke with him. Imagine his embarrassment and his surprise when they came to his gallery the night he was doing a showing for an artist—one of his *wife's* friends—to question him about a possible break in. Everybody was so appalled. And my friend was furious." I closed my eyes, pressed the tips of my fingers to my lids as the headache roared inside me, a dragon breathing fire inside my skull. "She claimed he was with *her* all morning. He'd been with her, off and on, for months. She consoled him, comforted him, and when I turned on him, she was there for him, too. She just loved to twist that knife."

Feeling hollow inside, I lowered my hands.

Jenks stood in the doorway, his hands shoved deep in his pockets, muscles bulging.

"He had an alibi. They let it go." I felt like I'd aged a hundred years as I pressed my head to the cool wall, letting it seep through to chill my overheated flesh. "So I installed cameras. When I moved, I did it again. And again here. Now…"

A chill rippled across my flesh.

Strong arms came around me. He kissed my neck, bared by my upswept hair. "Come home with me."

It seemed a simple answer.

It seemed terribly complicated.

It was both and it was neither.

"I don't really know you all that well, do I, Jenks?" I asked him, the question coming from me on a sigh.

"I'm not asking you to move in. Just until we figure out what to do from here. Where to go."

His hands settled on my hips and he rubbed his cheek against mine. "You know you're safe with me, right?"

That was one thing I did know.

But going home with him…

I wasn't so sure about that.

I couldn't stay here, though.

CHAPTER THIRTEEN

"**D**amn. Shadow. He's *hot*." Marla tipped her glasses down, studying Jenks over the tops of her lenses before pushing them back into place.

"I'll say." A wide, wicked grin lit Seth's face only to be replaced by a pained grimace as Marla jabbed an elbow into his ribs. "Hey, now, it's not fair you can go scoping him out if I can't."

She rolled her eyes. "Life ain't about fair, pal. Besides…" She shrugged and looked around. "It's not like *I* can compete with *that*."

Seth leaned in and hooked his arm around her neck, pressing a kiss to her mouth. "You don't need to. Even if he did swing both ways, he's not what I want. And that guy doesn't swing both ways, baby." Then he leaned back and shot me a wink. "Of course, if the two of you ever want to play…"

The blush was almost painful as it stained my cheeks. Focusing on my sketchbook, I propped my head on my hand. "Um…no. Whatever. No."

Seth laughed and pulled Marla into his lap, still grinning at me.

The sound of his laughter died and a moment later, they were both staring at me.

The amusement faded from Seth's blue eyes and he rested his chin on Marla's shoulder. The freckles there were more abundant than they had been a few weeks ago. Absently, he stroked his hand up and down her arm and my mind took a mental snapshot. *I'll draw them like that.* Maybe if it turned out, I could frame it and give it to them as a wedding gift.

I knew Seth, knew his moods, knew when something was weighing on him. And something *was* weighing on him. Putting my pencil down, I closed my sketchbook and reached for the rag, wiping the smudges from my fingers before glancing over to see if Jenks was still where he usually was.

He was actually farther away, leaving us alone, and he had his shades on, his T-shirt off, just staring out over the ocean. But yeah, there was no denying what Marla and Seth had said. He was hot.

Jenks lived about a half mile from there, a nice easy walk, and we'd made that nice, easy walk after he'd woken me up in bed…and he'd been inside me when I woke up.

It was a pretty decent way to start the day, even if it had caught me off guard.

My belly clenched just thinking about it and I ducked my head, hoping neither of them would notice the direction of my thoughts.

Marla laughed and I scowled. Wishful thinking.

"You went and fell hard, didn't you, honey?"

Groaning, I rested my forehead on the heel of my hand and stared out at the ocean.

"It's nothing like that," I said, but I knew it was a lie. I didn't know what Jenks and I were. But we were something.

"Then what's it like?" It was Seth who asked.

I couldn't exactly call Seth a girlfriend. He might be bisexual but he was still one of the most masculine men I'd ever met and there were some things you just can't confess to a man. But he was the first real friend I'd made in years. He was the person I trusted above all…even above Jenks.

Nervously, I flipped through my notebook, found the first portrait I'd drawn of Jenks. "The first time I saw him, I was just…looking for people to draw." I shrugged and flipped the spiral-bound pad of paper around, watched as they tipped their heads down to study it.

I'd let them see my work before. They were the only ones who had, aside from Jenks.

More than once, Marla had tried to convince me to take some of my portraits to a gallery run by a friend of hers. The answer was always no. It would remain no. This was mine. It would stay mine.

I watched as Marla reached up and stroked the tip of her finger down Jenks' back. He'd been sitting on the beach. That snarling wolf was the first thing I'd seen and it had caught my interest, captured it, held it.

"I've been drawing him for months." I shrugged and told them about the football, the terse conversation that followed, how I'd left my notebook.

And then, I waited. Part of me thought Marla was going to try to high-five me.

Instead, she dropped her head into her hands. "Fuck, Shadow. You... shit, I'm glad you two are getting along and all, but don't you think you should be more *careful?*"

I blinked.

Carefully, I reached for my sketches, extricating them out from under her elbows and then, pausing to study that first portrait of Jenks, I closed it, looked away. "Careful?"

"Some hot guy sees kinky pictures of you and you just go handing out your name. How do you know he's not a freak?"

The words hung there.

I looked down at my sketchpad, full of images that many, many people would describe as not quite normal. I thought of the way I checked my locks, once, twice, three times, thought of how I snuck out the back door to go to the beach, hoping my shadow wouldn't follow me.

I thought of my irrational need to make sure there was enough Aquafina in the house and how I couldn't sleep unless everything in my house was arranged just so.

"A freak," I whispered.

"Shadow, honey..."

Rising, I shook my head, gathering up my supplies. "I was married to a clean-cut, well-off type before. Belonged to one of the oldest families in Boston," I said. It took everything I had in me to keep my voice steady, to keep it level. "And he practically killed me."

I looked up as I delivered those final words, watched her flinch, saw the blood drain out of her face. "I think it's safe to say I've *been* married to a freak...and he turned me into one as well. Whatever I have going on with Jenks..." I stopped, sucked in a breath. I had to get myself under control because I felt like screaming. I didn't even know *why* I was suddenly so angry, but it was there, burning, bubbling under the surface. "Whatever it is going on, I don't know. But it's something real. It's something that makes me feel like I'm alive again."

Seth came off the table, reaching out. His fingers brushed my sleeve. "Shadow, wait."

I shot him a look. "Not right now."

"Marla didn't mean to hurt you." His eyes held mine. "We love you, you know that."

"Yes." I jerked my head in a nod. That was one thing I did know, one thing I did trust. "But I'm tired of hiding. I'm tired of living inside a bubble and I'm tired of protecting myself, having you all protect me. No, I don't know everything there is to know about Jenks, but I know that he doesn't make me shut down in fear and he's not trying to control me. That counts for something."

"It counts for a lot." He shot for a smile. It didn't quite reach his eyes. Marla had moved off the table and stood next to him, looking miserable. I didn't care.

I just wanted to get Jenks and leave.

The warmth of the sunshine, the peace of the ocean, had lost their appeal for me now.

"We just don't want you to get hurt." Seth held out his hand.

I caught his, squeezed. "I've already been hurt. What can anybody do to me than Stefan *didn't* do?"

Pulling the strap of my bag over my shoulder, I turned, headed down the beach. It felt odd. Walking this way. This direction didn't lead toward the false safety of my home.

It led toward Jenks and he was already on his feet, rising to meet me.

But nothing felt more right than when I put my hand in his.

His eyes glanced past me to study the table where I'd been sitting. I didn't know if Seth and Marla were still there or not. I didn't bother to look just then because I didn't care. Leaning in, I pressed my head to his chest and sighed, breathing in the scent of surf and sun and him.

"You want to head back to my place?"

"Yeah."

He nuzzled my neck, his fingers resting on my hip and I looked up, my lips parted to say something.

His gaze lowered, resting on my mouth.

And all the words inside my head died.

"Back to my place..." He murmured, his thumb slipping under the hem of my shirt. "When do you need to get to work?"

"*Ahhh...*" I blinked, tried to think. My computer hadn't been touched during the break-in and we'd spent last night setting it up in his spare bedroom. "By one." My voice was hoarse now and getting more ragged all the time.

"That's plenty of time, then."

"For what?"

A wicked grin lit his face. "You'll see."

I'd see...

Yeah, I could see, all right.

He sprawled out underneath me, the two of us tucked in the little *L* of his deck so that nobody from the beach could see us unless they actually came up *onto* the wooden planks.

Somehow, I didn't see them doing that.

Which was a good thing.

Exhibitionism wasn't a kink I wanted to indulge in.

All the fantasies I had, they needed to stay tucked inside my head, but Jenks had a way of reaching inside and pulling them out, one by one. This was straight from the pages of a sketchbook.

I'd imagined this, longed for it, drawn it…and now I had it.

He lay sprawled on his back, wearing absolutely nothing. Unless you counted me.

And I was fully dressed. I still wore my panties, but he'd pulled them to the side after he'd donned a rubber.

Now I sat atop him, my hands on his chest while he stared up at me.

"You look like a startled little fairy," he muttered, his hands gripping my hips.

Startled.

Was I startled?

I guess that was one word.

I felt startled.

I felt aching and hungry and needy as he surged up against me and he went so deep. His fingers spread wide to grip my ass and bring me down to meet each thrust and instinctively, I swayed forward. The friction had him *so* close to where I needed to feel him.

I did it again and he laughed, the sound rubbing against my skin.

He let go of my hip and reached up to catch my wrist. "You want it, take it," he said, his eyes burning into mine.

I blushed, felt the heat of it scalding my skin as he guided my hand between my thighs. Such a basic thing to do, touching myself. Such a basic thing, another piece of me, stolen away. I hadn't done this—

"Don't." His voice went hard, tight and the hand that had been guiding mine shot up into my hair, tightened. His grip was just this side of pain and I gasped, staring into his eyes as he sat up, watching me. Although I still straddled him, I felt surrounded by him. Lost in him. "You're sliding away from me again and you can't do that. Don't bring him here, not while I'm inside you. Not when your pussy is wet around me and I can feel you so close to coming."

Panic fluttered, tried to choke me.

"I can't always stop it—he finds a way in and I can't push him out," I said, forcing myself to speak.

"Then I will." He flipped us around and came down on top on me. When I would have pulled my hand away, he brought it back, staring at me, challenge written all over his face. His skin—dark and silken, stretched over muscles that rippled with every move—was hot against mine. "Touch yourself. You burn against me, you know that? I want to see what you like."

"You…" Blinking, I closed my eyes, the words hesitating in my throat. Then I forced myself to look back at him.

And he waited. Inside me, his cock throbbed, pulsed, but he hovered above me, one arm stretched out over my head, holding his weight easily, as if he would wait right there, forever.

"I barely remember what I like."

"Then it's time you find out." Slowly, his gaze bold and intent, he let it travel over me until he was staring at my hand. "I already know what you like…and you do, too. If you think about it. Now…show me. Show us both."

I felt a pulse shimmer through me as I slid my fingers against the hard, erect bud of my clitoris in a slow circle. I liked it when *he* did that. And I loved it when he toyed with me—fast, steady little strokes that brought me straight to the edge. I found that rhythm almost right away and cried out, my hips rocking in tight little circles, seeking to deepen the contact.

It wasn't enough.

I needed him deeper, and I needed it now. I needed—

"What?"

My gaze flew to his and I stared. Had I said that out loud?

I swallowed and realized yes. Yes, I had.

"You." One hand still clutched his shoulder and I slid it up, curved it around his neck as I watched him. "I need you. More than this…"

He surged against me and I arched up, crying out. "Like that?"

The only answer I could make was a whimper.

It was enough. He rocked against me, deep, hard strokes that had me bowing up off the chaise, my body straining to meet each thrust, my skin slicked with sweat, my heart pounding, all of me desperate for him.

And it still wasn't enough. I twined my legs around him, my arms clinging to him, and I cried out his name.

Then he swore, muttered mine as his hands gripped my ass and tucked me tight against him. His cock swelled, pulsed deep inside me and he shoved back and moved.

The hard, hot floor of the deck was against my back, my hair fanning out around me as he covered me. "Fuck, you're going to drive me nuts.

What are you doing to me?" he demanded, hooking an arm around my neck. He didn't give me a chance to answer and it wasn't as if I could have offered him one, anyway. His tongue drove into my mouth as his cock drove into me and nothing else mattered but him, his body, the way he possessed me.

That hard, driving, almost brutal possession.

And I loved, craved, needed every second of it.

He pounded into me and I sobbed out his name and came.

I wasn't sure what was more amazing—my climax, or the way he went rigid and snarled my name in the seconds before he orgasmed.

He left me alone in the cottage.

I nibbled my lip and studied the locks.

They weren't secure enough.

It was just a deadbolt and one of those flimsy old locks that all keyed doorknobs came with. A person could open that with that stupid bumping technique. It wasn't hard. I'd learned how to do it after I realized I had to know how vulnerable I was.

The answer? Very vulnerable.

It was *possible* Jenks had a lock that protected against bump keys, but who knew? A lot of people didn't realize how easy it was to break in.

Of course, that thought made me feel very, very stupid because I had the right locks, I had the security system and somebody had still managed to get inside.

How could I work here, though?

The door was too vulnerable. And the French doors that faced out over the beach were so exposed.

My belly twisted and I pressed my hands against my face. *Rational. Be rational. Think it through.*

That was what I had to do. That was how I coped.

Nobody but Seth and Marla knew where I was. Detective Barry had my number and she could probably figure out where I was, but none of Stefan's paid stalkers knew.

He wouldn't come here, would he?

My hands trembled as I dug my phone out of my pocket.

One thing to do, check and see what was going on with his gallery.

If he had a big show coming up, he'd be getting ready for it, not loitering around here. He was too much of a control freak and wouldn't trust anybody to handle the details leading up to a showing unless he was there to oversee things.

My heart kept racing away until the calendar loaded and then, the strength drained out of me, as if adrenaline was the only thing that had kept me upright as I saw the show he had lined up later this week.

No.

He wouldn't be here in South Carolina, not if Alessandra Shipley had the gallery. He'd wooed her for years, tried to pin her down and had finally done it just months before my life had gone to hell. He didn't let his assistants handle his big prizes and Alessandra was a big prize.

She was also one of the women he'd taunted me with. I couldn't hate her, though. Once, I might have. Now, staring at the image of her hauntingly lovely face, I just felt sad. I hoped he didn't hurt her as he'd hurt me.

He'd never be able do exactly what he'd done to me. If she disappeared for nine months, too many people would notice. Yes, he'd reported me missing, but after a time, the only people who'd even cared were the cops. It was easy to brush it aside.

Alessandra was a different story.

But Stefan knew a thousand ways to batter, all without leaving a mark. To tear into the body and show no sign.

He could destroy, and leave you broken, weeping inside, and nobody around you would ever be the wiser.

Closing the browser window, I tucked the phone away and stared at the door. I had to find the right way to make this settle in my head or I'd never get any work done.

But the question was...just how did I make my need for safety align with everything I saw as a risk?

Especially in a house that wasn't mine.

Jenks came home to find me sitting on the deck.

I hadn't been able to start work until three, which meant when seven rolled around, I wasn't able to stop. I usually only worked for six hours. The money my parents had left me allowed me a significant amount of freedom and I won't deny that I enjoyed it. When I needed to lose myself in work, I did just that, but I wasn't going to bind myself to deadlines and contracts, either. It could be another trap and I needed to have the freedom to do nothing, if I needed it.

Falling behind, though, wasn't an option, either.

For the past year, I'd built a reputation and I had people who'd come to count on me. For a girl who'd never had any measure of independence, that was something more precious than gold.

The current project was almost done. I felt a prickle of heat and looked up just as I started to put the finishing touches on the heroine's hair. Jenks was striding around the corner of the cottage. Moving fast, although not quite in a run. His face was grim, drawn tight, but when he saw me, something about him relaxed.

I gave him a tentative smile and shot a look into the house.

He already knew I was a basket case.

I guess it wasn't going to come as any surprise when he saw that I'd blocked the doors, was it?

Continuing to work as he mounted the steps, I stayed quiet.

He walked past me and I couldn't help but glance over my shoulder.

Couldn't help but feel foolish as he stopped in front of the French doors, staring inside. He could see clear through to the front door, could clearly see that I'd moved an armchair in front of the door—it was the closest heavy object that I could find. Then I'd put weights in front of it. As many of them as I could carry and he had a lot of free weights. That explained that very amazing body of his.

Looking back at the screen of my MacBook, I saw that I'd messed up the heroine's hair and I sighed. Better to stop now before I ruined it. It wasn't due for another week. I had time. I undid the damage, saved and then shut down, wrapping my arms around my legs as I waited for Jenks to come back to sit down.

It didn't take long.

He'd gone inside and I expected him to move everything back to its place, but in under two minutes, he was back out there, a Sam Adams in one hand, and an Aquafina in the other.

I took the water as he sat down on the low-lying coffee table in front of me.

"What's the problem?" he asked, his voice soft.

I jerked my gaze away. "Problem?"

"Shadow."

Reaching up, I worried the string that held the neckline of my shirt closed and focused on the water lapping at the shore. He was going to think I was crazy.

And it wasn't going to change no matter what I said. Sliding my gaze back to his, I shrugged and then said simply, "There aren't enough locks. I didn't feel safe."

Seconds passed and then he reached up, rubbed his hands across his face. He sat that way a long, long time. "It didn't seem to be an issue when I was here. Why is it when I'm not?"

"Because you're not." I pushed up and moved to stand at the railing. "You're asking for logic, Jenks. There isn't any and I can't make this logical. I can go visit Seth and Marla and if they are there, I don't think about the locks. When you're in my place, the locks aren't as much of an issue." I paused and looked down, an odd thought occurring. "I do check when it's Seth and Marla, though."

Turning, I rested against the railing and stared at him. "But if I'm alone, I have to know I'm safe. There aren't enough locks and the ones you have are terrible. I researched locks for three months before I found the right combination that I thought would keep me safe." The need to start fidgeting was strong, but I managed to just stand there and wait. "Those locks are awful. I could probably pick them."

His eyes came back to me, one brow arching up. "You can pick locks?"

"I can use a bump key." Now I had to do something. Unable to stand there, I moved over to the coffee table and took one of my sketchbooks, the one on the bottom. I was running out of paper, halfway through already and the extras I'd bought had been ruined. Time to buy more, but I didn't know where I'd keep them. Carry them with me? I didn't know. Flipping open to a blank sheet, I started to draw, letting my fingers guide me. And it was little surprise when Jenks' face started to take shape. It was him as he'd looked when I woke up last night, startled out of rest by the remnants of a dream. He'd only stayed asleep for a heartbeat after my eyes opened, but I had that image in my mind. Now I wanted it on paper.

"A bump key," he repeated.

"Yes, it's a key used for breaking into homes." I roughed out the image first. Best to do it that way, then go back and do the detail, shade in later.

"I know what a bump key is." He came over and sat down. His hands came up, gently.

I stilled, watched as he took my pencil from me, then the sketchpad, and set them aside. He grasped my waist, and easy as that, hauled me into his lap. "What I want to know is why you know, and more…how in the hell, and why in the hell, did you learn how to use one?"

The velvet of his eyes was too hard to look into, so I looked past him, staring out over the blue waters of the ever-changing ocean. Squirming around, I tucked my chin on his shoulder, aware of his chest rising and falling against mine. "It's hard to protect yourself until you know just how easy it would be for somebody to find you, hurt you," I finally said.

The arm he had wrapped around my waist tensed.

He tangled a hand in my hair and tugged.

Slowly, I let him guide my gaze to his and the probing stare he gave me left me feeling stripped and naked. "You're telling me you do shit like that so you know how easy it would be for him to get at you?" he demanded.

"How can I be safe if I don't?"

The hand in my hair spasmed.

His eyes squeezed shut.

Then, he crushed me against him and I couldn't do anything but stare out over the water while his chest heaved against mine. "I asked you once…" he said after almost ten minutes. His voice was ragged, edged with a growl and it sent a shiver down my spine. "I told you I wanted him dead in a ditch. I asked if you wanted him to be. Shadow, I'm having a hard time not making that into a reality right now."

I smoothed my hand up his neck, along his close-cut hair. "And if you get caught, what then?"

He leaned back. "I'd be damn sure not to get caught."

And judging by the look in his eyes, he knew what he was talking about.

"No." I shook my head, said it again, "No."

It was more important for me to have him there. He had somehow become too important to me.

"No." His eyes closed. A hard shudder went through him. Seconds ticked away. I could almost feel the slow, inexorable passage of time. When he looked back at me, the expression in his eyes was harsh, raw. Demanding. "Then trust me."

"Trust you?"

He pushed my skirt to my thighs. A second later, there was a jerk at my hips and he lifted me up.

"Trust me." He reached between us and then he was naked, the length of his cock bared and pressed against me. "I'll keep you safe."

Sensation jolted through me and I whimpered as his fingers sought me out, stroked me. It just took that, and I was ready. His eyes on me, a quick tug, and I was hungry, starving for him, wet and aching. "You might not always be here," I said, my voice shaking as he tucked the head of his cock against me.

"Yes." His eyes bored into me, practically daring me to say otherwise. "I will. Take me, Shadow."

I gasped as the fat head slid inside me. "You…" He was so hot. "You're not wearing a rubber."

"I know. You take the pill." He paused a moment, letting me think.

Slowly, I nodded. "I have to. Um…female reasons."

"Then unless you want me wearing one, we don't need it." He hesitated for another second. The hand in my hair slid to my face, cupped my cheek. "You'll be safe with me."

Those words, such a promise. Of so many things.

I let myself slide down against him. Such an intimate, deep connection. His hands caught my hips under my skirt. His mouth pressed to my neck. "Shadow."

I shivered. He trailed one finger along the crevice between the cheeks of my bottom and I stilled, my eyes seeking his face. "Stay with me," he ordered, taking my mouth as he started to move within me.

There was no question of that. Not this time. Driving so deep inside me, stretching me, so hot, and I felt so much *more*—he was like silk stretched over iron and each stroke was a delicious, shuddering little tease. Too much, far too much sensation, and I was lost.

Lost…and I was perfectly fine with it.

As he came inside me, bringing me to climax, his mouth caught mine and my climax was a desperate cry against his lips.

Safe. And with him.

Two things I desperately needed.

CHAPTER FOURTEEN

I had a week of bliss.

Maybe the locksmith looked at me as if I were crazy when I told him the exact kind of locks I wanted on each door, but the look faded fast when he looked at Jenks, standing so close behind me.

Something inside me whispered that I was rushing things, and logically, I even understood that.

But I couldn't go back home, not yet.

I'd tried, for one night.

And I'd panicked every time I heard a loud sound.

I'd never feel safe there again.

Detective Barry had told me that my ex-husband had an alibi for the night my home was vandalized. So shocking. The alibi? A former friend of mine, Lesil Holland. She was his administrative assistant and they had been *otherwise engaged*. Barry had a dry tone in her voice when she told me that, and I had a feeling she was using the exact tone Lesil had used when the woman had given the alibi.

Lesil could have lied.

She could have done so easily.

And none of it mattered.

I'd expected nothing more, really.

What *did* matter? I had a place where I felt safe and now there was a series of locks that I could actually trust. The French doors were a problem, but Jenks promised me they were solid and strong and he was going to look into having an alarm system installed that would trigger an alert if windows were broken. I could work with that. And he was home at night. During the day, I could work outside where there were people and if there were people, I was safe.

I had a week of what was almost paradise, for me. I even managed a few days where I only checked those locks twice after Jenks left each day at two. He was gone from two until almost nine, working, Monday through Friday, and I managed to get caught up and even get some stock covers done. Then I went to upload them on my site and I couldn't.

What was worse…when I went to log in, the site was locked to me.

My heart lunged up into my throat and I automatically went to my website to make sure it was up and a scream rose in my throat at what I saw.

Swiping out with my arm, I knocked the MacBook from my lap and watched as it crashed to ground. Limbs lose and shaking, I clambered to my feet and stumbled away.

I recognized myself.

Others probably wouldn't, but I did.

The skinny arch of my spine, bent over.

He'd used an infrared camera or whatever it was that allowed one to take pictures in the dark. Was that how he had always found me so easily?

I didn't know.

I was naked, bent over. A puddle of something wet, dark and shiny spread out from under me and I shoved the back of my fist against my mouth to keep from screaming.

How had he gotten to my website?

I grabbed my phone, called Seth.

He'd helped me set it up, still helped with updates. If anybody could help, it would be him.

▲▼▲

"Son of a fucking *bitch*!" Seth snarled as he slammed a fist against the table.

I flinched.

Marla wrapped an arm around my shoulders and rubbed her cheek against my hair.

"He has to get it down," I said, my voice shaking.

It had been three hours. I didn't know how much longer I could handle it, seeing that image, knowing others had seen it.

"He will."

Silence fell once more, broken only by the *ratta tat tat* of Seth's fingers flying over the keys and his short, terse sentences as he spoke with tech support. He used local places for everything and that made some of it easier. It also meant that somebody might be able to connect that broken, pale form on my website to me.

"Yeah…yeah…" Seth paused. "Got it."

A few seconds later, he hung up the phone and then hunched over the keyboard. While he was banging away, the first of the series of locks on the door unlocked.

He didn't look up.

Marla and I did.

Jenks stood in the doorway.

The silence that fell was one of those awkward, almost heavy silences. So heavy, I'd think we couldn't lift it. My throat burned and ached as I huddled against Marla, her arm a comforting weight around my shoulders.

Jenks slid his gaze over to Seth, lingered there before coming back to me as he came inside and shut the door at his back. "What's going on?"

Marla looked at me as I straightened up. I had to handle this. Even as she opened her mouth, I knew what she was going to say. But I had to do this. Shaking my head, I said, "No."

Seth shot a look over his shoulder at me, then Marla, his gaze barely glancing over Jenks. "Marla, leave her be. She can handle this," he said. Then he went back to the computer. Or started to. His gaze bounced past Jenks, then came back, hesitated.

Jenks looked at him, stared.

Something about that look made my belly draw tight, but I didn't have time, or the soul left inside me, to panic about whatever had Seth looking like that, and the heart-destroying image I'd seen on the computer.

My legs felt clumsy beneath me as I shoved upright. I don't know if gravity had increased or if I was just that tired, but it was so hard to stand there, so hard to look at him as I asked Seth, "Is it still up?"

I felt my friend's eyes on me as he said softly, "No. I got it down right before he walked in. I've…" He paused.

I looked over at him, waited.

"There are screen shots." His brows dropped low over his eyes as he stared at me. "You don't need to show him, Shadow. Just tell him."

"You said it yourself." My voice shook as I reminded him. "I can handle this."

His angry, ugly curse blistered the air as he shoved his hands through his spiked hair, dyed black as the night. Then he tapped a few keys and brought the images up. "There." He jerked his chin up and stood, glaring at Jenks.

Something angry and tight stretched out between them. I didn't know what it was, couldn't understand it, and it didn't matter. I'd deal with that later. After…after this. What the hell.

Jenks walked across the floor, his steps oddly rigid, his spine tense. One hand hung at his side, curled into a fist. He stopped in front of the monitor and then he whipped his head around, stared at me. "What the flying fuck? What is this?"

"That was me," I said, my voice wooden. "Three years ago, give or take. Some time before the tornado."

His eyes went icy. A muscle bunched in his jaw. "How?"

"I…" My voice broke. Looking away, I managed, somehow, to get the words out even though it felt like my heart, my soul, was dying, shriveling away inside me. "He must have used some sort of infrared camera. That was me, that was how I looked when I got to the hospital. Skin and bone, maybe a week or two away from death. He took pictures of me like that. And he kept them."

"How did you get them?" he demanded.

I looked back at them and then turned away. "Seth?"

"Somebody hacked her website," Seth said, his voice hard and lined with iron. "Everything is gone. I've got it backed up on my hard drive at home, but instead of the portfolios and everything we spent months setting up, there's just this."

He flipped the screen off and stormed away, moving to stare out the window a few feet away from me, his body vibrating with fury. "Son of a *bitch*."

"Seth…"

"I'm sorry, Shadow."

I closed my eyes and pressed my brow to the glass.

"It's not your fault."

"Fuck that. I designed the site, set up the security and somebody got through." He spun back around and glared at the computer on the other side of the room. He looked at it as if he thought it might come alive and devour us.

Personally, I thought that might be the easier way to go.

But death by monsterized computer equipment didn't happen in the next few minutes and I had to watch as Jenks bent over the computer, his hands braced on the desk, that muscle still pulsing in his jaw. He scrolled through the screen caps, including the ones where Seth had taken shots of the IP number and everything else he could track down.

"They have no idea who requested the password reset?" he asked after almost five minutes.

"No, genius," Seth bit off, his voice sour. "If they did, I could be a lot more useful."

Jenks slowly lifted his head, turned and stared at Seth across the long, gleaming expanse of polished wooden floor.

Seth jerked his chin up and crossed his arms over his chest, glared right back.

"Seth."

He looked over at me, the moment shattering around them. I had to fight to keep from sucking in a breath as the tension in the room ebbed away and the testosterone levels returned to something resembling normal. "What?" he bit off.

"What did the tech people say?"

Some of the fury drained away, replaced by frustration and he turned back to the windows, staring outside. "It was an online request. They'll get us what info they can, but whoever requested the password had the security info and nothing set off the red flags. We wouldn't be having this conversation if anything had triggered any alerts."

"Stefan isn't a computer person." I felt as though somebody had reached inside and tied me into knots—hot, tight painful ones. I wanted to crawl away somewhere and hide. I wanted to run. I wanted the floor to open up beneath me and just swallow me whole. Fear, humiliation and horror washed over me in awful waves.

Hands came up and covered my shoulders.

I tensed, the urge to jerk away from Jenks grabbing me hard.

He must have sensed it because he crowded up against me and wrapped his arms around me, one bracketing my upper arms, the other coming around my waist. In the back of my mind, a wild, terrified voice started to scream as memories broke free.

I focused on the dying rays of the sun as it sank into the water, the rays of gold and orange turning the waves to fire. I wasn't trapped in darkness. This wasn't Stefan. The scents that surrounded me were of musk, man, the ocean and the sun. I wasn't choking on the overpowering scent of sandalwood—some customized cologne Stefan had always worn. That cologne had come to signal despair. I wouldn't find myself shoved to the floor, pinned down and battered, beaten, violated yet again.

Breathing through my teeth, I looked down at his arms. Slowly, I lifted one hand, stroked my fingers along his arm.

Some of the tension I felt in him relaxed.

"You don't think it was anybody but him, do you?" he asked, his voice low. Seth heard, but Marla, still a good fifteen feet away didn't.

I turned my head, met his gaze, so close to mine. I breathed in, let the familiar scent of him sooth me. "It was him. He would have paid some-body—he couldn't do it and wouldn't bother to learn, assuming he could, but it was him."

"Then there's a trail."

That heavy silence returned.

I hated it, could have screamed, just to shatter it.

As my heart throbbed and raced like a wild thing, I had to fight the urge to pace the floors. My chest felt tight and hot. The sun was barely a sliver on the horizon now and the thought of the daylight being gone, of being wrapped in darkness once more, made my lungs go tight.

Dimly, I heard Jenks speaking and I had to force myself to listen. He wasn't even speaking to me.

"Anything else you can do?"

Seth's lip curled as he stared at Jenks. The antipathy between them was palpable and I didn't understand it. I needed to but it was one more thing that my brain just couldn't process.

"Sure, big guy," Seth drawled, his voice heavy, all but dripping with sarcasm. Then he cut his gaze my way and his eyes softened. He dragged his hands down his face and looked back out over the water. "I'll ramp up the security, add as many layers as I can. Maybe the tech guys can suggest some stuff. They're going to get with me as they learn what happened anyway."

"What do they expect to find?" I shook my head, vaguely aware I'd leaned back against Jenks. It wasn't unpleasant, I realized, letting him hold me like this. It was an embrace, not a prison. That wasn't a bad thing. His breath teased the hair at my temple, his hand covered my breastbone protectively.

"I don't know. They can at least pinpoint where the mess started, what part of the country." Seth shrugged "That's not much, but it's something. And they may be able to find more."

"I want more." Jenks' voice was hard, full of an authority I hadn't heard from him before."

Seth glared at him. "Yeah, well, I'd like to tell you to suck my dick, but we know how that will go over, don't we?" Then he looked at me.

Jenks stiffened.

"Don't." I broke away, placed myself between them. "I don't know what is with you two, but don't. Okay?"

Then I turned, stormed out of the room. Ahead of me, the bedroom loomed, the doorway a dark maw. I slapped at the wall inside clumsily until the lights came on. The soft golden glow wasn't enough to chase away the shadows. Not tonight.

Tonight, I didn't know if anything would work to ease the horror inside.

The four walls threatened to close around me and, desperate, I shoved through the French doors, throwing them open and lurching outside.

Turning on the sconces on the wall, I stumbled over to the fire pit and managed to get it lit. The flames blazed to life, but did nothing to warm me inside.

Time crawled by.

It could have been five minutes since I came outside, desperate to escape.

It could have been fifty.

When the door opened, I closed my eyes and would have stayed that way if I hadn't felt the weight of their stares, boring into me.

Anger and nerves were etched on Seth's face and Marla looked uneasy. She held his hand, but something about the way they touched had me thinking she was holding him *back*. Seth, one of the most easy-going guys I knew.

"You okay here?" Seth asked, the words tumbling out of him so fast, I barely understood him.

Jenks moved out of the bedroom but didn't come any closer, a dark shadow hovering just outside that circle of light. My gaze locked on him and I tried to understand just what was going on.

I didn't know and that hot ball in my chest surged and expanded. "Why wouldn't I be?" It came out rougher than I expected, almost ragged, and I looked back at the fire, tried to find some measure of peace.

"You can come home with us," Seth offered. "You won't be alone there."

Marla leaned against him, her head against his arm. Her eyes met mine. "You're always welcome, baby. You're like a sister to me."

"You need to find a better family tree," I said softly. Then I shook my head. "No. I appreciate it, but no. Stefan's already tried to ruin Seth's life. It won't take much for him to decide to fuck around with you, too. I love you all too much to let him make you a target because you were kind to me."

I smoothed my skirt around my knees, idly wondering what it said that I didn't worry so much about Jenks in that regard. But I didn't worry about

Stefan coming after Jenks. He'd even left Seth alone once he realized he wouldn't be able to push that man around. He'd tried, he'd failed. Marla, though...I shivered.

He hadn't tried to go after her, and I didn't want to give him a reason to shift his attention that way.

Smoothing my fingers across my skirt, I stared at my knees. "No," I said again. "You two can go home. I'll be fine here."

Seth hesitated. Marla sighed. Then she came toward me, bent down to hug me. "Call if you need me. We'll be in touch."

"I know." I pressed my face to her hair, breathed in the scent of the pear and vanilla shampoo she so loved. "Kick Seth in the knee for me. He's oozing testosterone all over the place."

"He's just worried." She brushed my hair back, kissed my cheek. Then she turned back, gave Seth an odd look.

He ignored her and came over. He crouched down in front of me and caught my hands, eying me strangely. The intent, almost angry look in his eyes unsettled me. "You call when you need me."

Not if...

That bothered me.

A lot.

Then abruptly, he leaned in and grabbed me, held me tightly. "You need to get that son of a bitch to tell you the truth, Shadow," he said, his voice low and urgent, just a bare whisper that only the two of us heard.

Then, before I could even figure that out, he was gone, catching Marla's hand and striding past Jenks without sparing the other man so much as a glance.

Jenks didn't even seem to notice.

His eyes rested on me.

And as he came my way, that heat inside my chest expanded even more. I felt as though I had a volcano inside me and it was threatening to erupt.

"You want to tell me what is going on with the two of you?" I demanded.

He was quiet.

I surged up out of the seat and started to pace, unable to stay still. I'd left the bedroom because I felt trapped.

Being outside should make it better, but it didn't.

It could be the darkness or maybe it was the walls within my own mind, closing in around me.

Desperate to escape whatever prison had me feeling like this, I stalked back and forth along the railing, my skirt tangling around my legs, my skin icy even as that volcano in my chest tried to burn me.

"Are you going to talk to me?" I asked when I whipped around and saw Jenks in my path.

I thumped my fist against his chest and the anger that broke out over me, catching me in a tight, ruthless grip caught me completely off guard. Slamming my palms against his chest, I snarled at him. "Damn it, Jenks."

His hands caught my wrists.

I went still.

"Your friend is an ex-con," he said quietly.

Frozen, I stared up at him, his face caught half in the shadow, half in the light of the fire. It was an eerie depiction and the anger inside me quieted. It didn't fade, but it went silent as I realized something life-shattering was about to happen.

I just might need that anger even more in a minute.

Twisting out of his reach, I backed away. "Yeah? So what?"

"You knew."

"Yes." I swiped my hands down my skirt, painfully aware of the fact that I was shaking. *Shaking.* I hated that I felt like this. That Jenks had made me feel like this. "He told me. That was how Stefan thought to use him—he had a record, and Stefan thought it made him an easy mark. Seth came to me. He fucked up, got his life on track. Doesn't make him a bad person."

Jenks looked down, his gaze on his feet. Wide shoulders rose and fell. "I hope you remember that, sugar. Fuck, I hope you remember that." Then he turned away. Over his shoulder, he said, "Wait here."

Wait here.

He disappeared into the bedroom, but he wasn't gone for more than a minute before he returned, carrying something in his hand. "People sometimes lie," he said. "Most of the time, it's for bullshit reasons. Other times, they have to. I didn't have much choice."

Then he extended his hand and I stared at what he held out for a long, long time before it made sense.

When it finally did, I turned away.

CHAPTER FIFTEEN

My legs didn't want to work.

Clutching at the railing made it easier to stand, but I couldn't clutch at the railing and still walk into the cottage and pack. It didn't work out.

My brain wouldn't stop spinning.

And I thought maybe my heart was withering inside my chest.

"You're a cop."

Well. That's a brilliant observation, I thought as he remained silent behind me.

I continued to cling to the railing as awful sobs built inside me. I wanted to turn around and throw myself at him, beat him, bloody that beautiful face of his, but there was no point.

Although the reasons for it had yet to come out, one thing was clear. Jenks had lied to me.

Now I just wanted to understand why.

Once I did that, I could maybe get my leaden legs to work and then I could drag myself out of there.

My voice trembled as I forced the words out, "Tell me."

And all I got was more silence.

The volcano erupted.

There was a pretty glass hurricane lamp on one of the tables and I didn't even remember grabbing it, much less throwing it. But I remember seeing it smash into the wall, seeing the shards flying. I remember seeing the surprise on his face as he looked at me.

"Shadow—"

There was a bottle of water on the table. Not much else, but he always managed to make sure there was a bottle of water any place I might be and I always ended up out here. The bottle went flying next and then I was caught against him, his hips pinning mine to the wooden railing at my back, his hands capturing my wrists. "Stop," he whispered, his voice ragged. "Just stop. I'll tell you."

But I didn't want to stop.

Somewhere inside me, there had been a kernel of rage and he'd just managed to expose it.

As he leaned in, pressed his brow to mine, I struck out, sinking my teeth into his lip, so hard I broke the skin.

He jerked back but said nothing.

I kicked him. My foot was bare and it hurt me more than him, but I didn't let that stop me.

His hands fell away from my wrists and I made a fist, striking out.

He took that hit, and another.

Then I reached up. Caught his face.

He stared at me, his eyes unreadable.

When I pulled his face to mine, he came.

Anger surged and hurt burned. Underneath it all, that need was still there. They all danced around and the lust that exploded through me was more than I could handle. This time, I was the one to trace his lips with my tongue. I was the one to tear his jeans open and free his cock.

"Damn you," I muttered, tears burning my eyes as he sank inside me, my hips braced against the railing.

"I know." He held me open and his hands were gentle.

Gentle wasn't what I wanted or what I needed. I bit him again and tightened my knees around him. "Don't be nice right now." I glared at him and pulled myself closer, wrapping myself against him.

He stilled, staring at me.

And then he lifted me, turned.

A moment later, I was caught between him and the wall. Glass crunched under his boots and I didn't care. I felt like there were shards of it driving into my heart with each thrust but nothing mattered. For now, there was this. It was the one thing that *was* real. He *did* want me.

Maybe all he wanted was sex and everything else was a job, but he did want me.

That counted for something...it had to.

I locked him out of the bathroom.

I needed to be alone for a few minutes.

Part of me wanted to find a way out of there. Maybe go to the airport and just run away. Forever.

I could do it.

I had everything I needed. I had my passport, money in the bank. If I took my MacBook, I could work from anywhere and set up in another town, another state, another country if I had to.

On legs that shook, I climbed into the shower, pummeled by memories of that first time we were there. It all felt so real. As though he cared. As though he wanted me. No, it went deeper than that. Felt like something so much more. He was already in my blood, in my soul and I could have sworn he felt the same. Was it all lies?

Soap suds ran into my eyes, blinding me and I let myself pretend for a minute that was why the tears started to run. I didn't take comfort in the lie for long, and I didn't let myself cry for very long, either. That volcano in my chest had emptied itself and now all that remained was ash. I felt hollow, empty.

After I'd washed, I climbed out and then stood there, lost and staring at nothing. I had no clothes, except the dirty ones I'd left in a pile by the sink and I couldn't tolerate the idea of putting them on. They would smell of him, and they'd feel of lies and brokenness and desolation.

Instead, I wrapped myself in a towel and slid out of the room.

He'd talked me into putting my clothes away, hanging up my skirts, some of the shirts, using the empty space in his dresser for my panties and bras. Now as I pulled out the drawer and grabbed a clean set of lingerie, I wondered why I had bothered.

The floorboards creaked behind me but I didn't turn around.

Cool air danced across my skin as I dropped the towel. I felt his eyes on my back as I donned the panties, a bra. As I turned to go to the closet, he stared at me, hands in his pockets. My gaze skated past his. I didn't want to see him, talk to him. Nothing.

I'd have to, but I didn't want it to be *now*. There was no hope for it, though. I'd have to talk to him. See him. Deal with him.

Clothes first. I'd feel better once I was dressed.

None of the long skirts or drapy shirts looked right. My hand landed one of his shirts, a simple black button-down and I grabbed it. My heart gave a single, hard bump against my ribs as his scent surrounded me, but I ignored it. A new start, maybe. It was time for a new start.

I shoved my arms into the sleeves and buttoned it up before I looked at him.

"I want to know why," I said, surprised at how firm my voice was, how solid I sounded.

"Why what?"

I snorted, and it caught us both off guard. He'd talked me into putting my clothes away, but now, in the frustration, I couldn't find them. I jerked drawers open until I did. I pulled out a pair of jeans and donned them, buttoning them and turning to glare at Jenks. "You know *why*. You had a reason, you son of a bitch. Why the fuck did you decide to use me?"

That caught his attention.

He came off the wall and prowled toward me, his eyes narrowed, one hand clenched into a tight fist.

He reached up to touch me and I jerked back.

He froze, his hand lingering there in midair before he stopped, dropped it to his side.

"I never used you," he said, his voice taut.

"Oh, please." Too much, I realized.

It was too much. I had a fleeting memory of watching as the earth was shoveled over my parents' coffins—it had started then, maybe. That was when I started letting things trap me, although it had been quiet, subtle little things. My aunt hadn't loved me and I'd known it, tolerated it because I hadn't had to live there for long. I'd stayed in my room, kept quiet, pretended that I hadn't even existed, just so I wouldn't have to fight with her. Stefan—he had made me *think* he had loved me, but even from the beginning, he had made me change what I was.

Who I was, even. I couldn't be *Shadow*. The flighty, weird name my mother had given me wasn't appropriate. I had to be Grace. My laugh had been too loud. I wouldn't even recognize the sound of it now. Even on the rare occasion that I *did* laugh, my laugh was…broken, just like my voice. Just like me, in many ways. I was remaking myself, but I'd never be the same.

I forced myself to look at Jenks. "What do you *want?*" I snarled, anger, a living, breathing beast in my chest, pulsing and throbbing like a wild thing.

His eyes held mine.

"I don't want anything now that I didn't want a week ago, two hours ago." He took one step.

I tensed.

He turned away, biting off a curse. "Why the fuck are you afraid of *me?*"

"I'm not *afraid* of you." And it was the truth. Imagine that. I could actually look at him and say that and mean it. I waited until his gaze came back to mine. "I'm pissed off and I'm hurt and I'm confused…and I can't *trust* you. You won't tell me what's going on, Jenks. Damn it. What is going on?"

His mouth opened. Closed.

But in the end, he didn't say anything.

I nodded, my heart cracking. Then I turned back and finished packing. "Whatever it is, I hope it's important."

I guess it was. Somewhere deep inside, a part of me realized one crucial thing. He did care about me. Later on down the road, that might help. Some. But it didn't help right now.

The only thing that was going to help was the one thing I was already doing.

I was packed in under twenty minutes. It would have only taken fifteen, but I had to stop and call a cab.

I didn't know where to go.

I'd lived on Pawley's Island for nearly three years now. It wasn't far from the more populated areas of Myrtle Beach, but I rarely ventured outside my safe zone.

I had no idea where to go.

The cab driver gave me an odd look as I told him to just drive around.

I guess he didn't get too many people who didn't care about that running meter, but I needed to think and I didn't care that the meter was running.

After twenty minutes of just driving, watching as that fare went higher and higher, I pulled out my phone and started a search. I couldn't go back home. For the very same reasons as before, Seth and Marla's place was out of the question.

But I couldn't spend the rest of my life in the back of a cab, either. Especially not one that smelled of French fries, one of those tree-shaped air fresheners, and too much Old Spice. A search for hotels near Pawley's Island led me to a travel site and the very first one was a very pricey hotel that boasted beautiful views of the bay and my heart clutched a little as I saw it.

Beautiful.

It was beautiful. It was also perfect.

It was a drive, closer to Myrtle Beach, but that wasn't a problem.

Without thinking twice, I called.

There were rooms available and that was all I needed to know.

The cab driver looked relieved to have a destination in mind and I was relieved to be out of the car, some thirty minutes later. It was past eleven and I needed to close my eyes, put my head on a pillow, even if I didn't sleep.

Somehow, someway, I'd figure out what to do, where to go from here.

Because I knew they'd worry, I sent Seth and Marla a text.

Not staying with J. Asked him the truth. He told me. Left and went to a hotel. I need a few days. I'll call.

That was it.

Short and sweet.

Part of me wanted to call Seth and yell at him. Damn him to hell, but if he'd kept his mouth shut, I could have lived in blissful ignorance for a good long while.

It wasn't his fault, though.

My chest ached and I rubbed the heel of my hand over the hole where my heart had once been.

A few months ago, I'd wanted to wake up. Feel alive again.

Now I just wanted to go back to the numb solitude where I'd existed for so long. What had I been thinking? It was so much easier, I thought, to feel nothing.

The view from the room *was* beautiful.

The room itself was beautiful.

I thought maybe I could use it as inspiration and maybe just stay there for a long, long time. I could draw the city, draw the people walking by. Maybe stay for a week or two, a month. I had the money. I needed to rethink my life.

No. I needed to *get* a life. I didn't have one now. I scrambled to pick up whatever excess emotions that I could and I clung to the man who'd shown me kindness, but was that really a life?

Kindness.

Even as I tried to insist that was the word I needed, another part of me processed it and then threw it back at me, laughing hysterically.

What Jenks had shown me went a lot deeper than *kindness*.

"Do you really think he's just been engaging in pity fucks?" I muttered, turning away from the jewel-toned lights of the skyline. Myrtle Beach was almost drab during the day, but at night, it came to life.

The beautiful room spread out before me and I collapsed on the bed, hugging a pillow to my chest.

No. It was more, and I knew it. But it was so hard to understand what it was when he wouldn't talk to me.

Maybe I should push the issue.

If I mattered, and I thought I did, I should make it clear he either had to talk to me, now...well. Not this minute *now*, but within a reasonable time frame, or it was just over.

I'd pack up, move on. I loved Pawley's Island but I could find another place to love. I'd miss Seth and Marla, but that wasn't enough to hold me there. Especially since Stefan was starting to harass me.

I needed something else.

Something more.

I started to reach for my phone, but in the end, I settled on the little balcony with my laptop. It would be easier to think this through if I wrote it all out in an email. Then I wouldn't have to wait and hold my breath on an immediate answer, anyway.

Easier that way, all around.

Already thinking it through, I logged in to my email.

I didn't pay attention to the all the emails I had in my inbox. The number made me wince, but I'd mentally been preparing for it—the horror of that picture on my site was going to cause some sort of response and plenty of friends and colleagues would be checking on me. None had my phone number—I didn't trust anybody enough to give them that, but they'd get in contact however they could.

I didn't skim through them. I just opened a new email and started to write.

Dillian,
We need to talk. If you decide not to talk to me, that's answer enough and I'll just close up the house. I don't think this is the place for me anymore.
If you do want to talk to me, you'd better be—

I stopped, rubbed my brow and got up to pace, unsure of what I wanted to say, what I needed to say.

Three minutes of internal debate didn't make the words flow any easier so I returned and forced them out, one by one.

You have to give me some kind of answers here. If you don't, or even if you can't, I guess that is answer enough. I had everything from my name and my voice and my choice stripped away. I won't be made into nothing again, and you deceiving me makes me feel like nothing. I can't do this. Either you talk to me or it's just over. I realize that might feel unfair, but I deserve more than that.

I'll be at my table until noon Wednesday. If you're not there, I guess it's done.

A part of me feels like I'm falling in love with you. But I can't do that if I don't know who you are.

S.

I read it through twice.

Since there was nothing else to say, I sent it before I could lose my nerve.

Then I leaned back in the chair and rubbed my eyes.

I made myself stare into the velvety black that lay over the ocean, waited for the punch of fear to come, but it didn't. Maybe I could beat some of it back after all.

Minutes passed and an odd sort of acceptance rolled over me. It wasn't peace. I couldn't be at peace in the dark, not with everything going on, but I wasn't terrified, and come what may with Jenks, I wasn't going to roll over and just take it anymore, either.

I was so done with—

The phone chimed.

I frowned.

That was a ring I hadn't heard in ages.

Tony?

Man, I hadn't heard from him in a while. I bumped into him every now and then in town, but we rarely had anything to say to each other. With a frown, I read the message on my screen.

Got time to talk? Feeling kind of blue lately about Seth. Don't know who else to talk to.

Tony wasn't exactly one of my favorite people in the world, but I wasn't really feeling ready to go bed, either.

Blowing out a sigh, I typed out, *sure*. Then hit send.

As I waited for the phone to ring, I went back to email and mentally groaned as everything started to load.

The email at the very top caught my attention. Held it. Almost numb, I answered the phone more out of habit than anything else.

CHAPTER SIXTEEN

"**G**race," Tony said, his voice soft. "It's been a long time."

My skin went cold, tight. *Grace.* Why was he calling me *Grace?*

Still staring at that picture, I swallowed "Hasn't it? How are you?"

I enlarged the picture. Stared at Marla's face, the gag. There was a hand in her hair, jerking her head back. I knew from experience, it would be painful. What I didn't know was who stood behind her, or who took the picture. What I didn't know was where Seth was.

Or why Tony had called me *Grace.*

"Kicking my own ass. A lot. I never should have left Seth. Never should have fought with him like I did. He was right, you know. Standing up for you like he did. I should have done the same, should have stayed by him." He was quiet a moment and then softly, he added, "I miss you two. I...I hear he's planning to get married."

Planning.

"Yes. Marla's wonderful." I kept my voice neutral.

"I bet," Tony said sourly. "He gets to pretend he's nice and normal, just like he always wanted."

"All Seth ever wanted was to be happy. Marla gives him that."

Tony was quiet. "Yeah. Yeah, I guess. Listen...can...maybe I can come over. I just need to talk. This phone shit doesn't work. Are you at home?"

My skin went tight, started to crawl and it had nothing to do with that picture of Marla. I checked the time stamp. It had been sent today. Maybe two hours after they left Jenks' house. I couldn't see much of her clothing, but the strap of her shirt looked to be the same one she'd had on earlier. The earrings, too.

"I'm not at home," I said softly. "There was a problem at my house a few days ago. I…I guess I could meet you at Seth and Marla's. I won't be able to be there for a good two hours, though. Guess it's a good thing I'm such a night owl, huh?"

Tony flat-out loved that idea.

I hung up the phone. I stared at Marla's picture. Then I called Seth.

The phone rang for a very long time.

But there was no answer.

I wanted to cry.

Instead, I called another number.

Jenks answered almost immediately.

I told him what I needed to say, and then, as he yelled at me, I hung up.

I knew what Tony was up to, and I knew why.

It had nothing to do with Seth, with Marla, or even Tony.

Somehow, Stefan was behind this.

It took forty minutes to get to the street where I'd once felt safe.

Once.

No longer.

The monster that had stripped me of my life, my name, even my voice for a time had managed to come back in and strip me of my safety. He'd touched my life, yet again, and I wanted to bloody him for it. I wanted to hurt him. The fury inside me had blasted me into wakefulness and I realized that it wasn't going to subside.

I'd wanted to wake up.

I had my wish.

As I'd asked, the cab driver let me out one street ahead and I moved in behind Seth and Marla's house, taking the alley that most of the people on that side of the street used to access the narrow parking slots for their cars, assuming they *had* cars. Staying in the shadows, I found Seth and Marla's little place and stopped.

It was dark.

Dark and quiet and my skin crawled as I stared up at it.

Going inside was going to take every bit of courage I had and I wasn't sure I had enough.

But I had to look.

Maybe the picture had just been a really, really good piece of photo-shopping. I hadn't thought to look because I'd been so freaked. Maybe it was something Seth and Marla were into and I didn't need to know about their kinks.

And maybe I would wake up tomorrow feeling like Xena, Warrior Princess.

One step. If I could just do one step.

I lifted my foot—

And almost screamed as a hand shot out and closed around my arm from behind me.

As the shadow in the darkness whirled me around, I struck out, fighting and clawing. I wouldn't go back, I wouldn't—

Jenks caught my wrist. "It's me."

His voice, low and steady, penetrated the fog, but not immediately. I struck him a second time and was almost ready to go for a third before the words made sense.

The street lights were enough to see his face.

They were also enough for me to see the badge he had hanging around his neck and I paused, swallowing at the sight of it.

"What..." I backed away, looking down the alley. "Why are you here?"

From the corner of my eye, I saw the look on his face and I realized I sounded as though I'd lost my mind. Had I really called him *just* to inform him that I thought Stefan had somehow managed to get Seth's former lover to spy on me, talk him into...what, exactly?

I'd called him, I realized belatedly, because I did trust him.

What that meant for us, I didn't know.

Yet.

But he was here because I trusted him, because I could trust him.

Looking back at the house, I said, "Stefan's done something to Marla. And more than likely, Seth, too."

"You don't know that." He pushed something into my hand and I looked down to see a set of keys. "My car. It's at the end of the block, a black Mustang. Get in. Lock the door."

I looked up at him blankly. "Are the police here?"

"I *am* the police."

"You're one police...officer. Whatever."

He muttered something and then pointed. "Would you *go?*"

I stared down the dark maw of the alley, all the shadows looking like hungry demons, ready to suck me into hell. "No. If Stefan has anything to do with this, he's more than likely around somewhere watching. I don't think *alone* is the ideal thing anyway."

Not to mention that whatever was going on was because of me. Yes. It was stupid, and yes, it was foolish, but I was the reason this was happening. I had to see it through.

Besides, my gut whispered that Stefan wasn't here.

He'd brought Tony in a for a reason.

He never did like to get his hands dirty.

I was still trying to process why I'd gotten the pictures of Marla *before* Tony had made that call, but I'd work that out later.

"You're not going in there," Jenks said, his voice implacable.

"Well, I'm not going to a car, either." I glared at him, fighting the urge to do something stupid and childish, like kick his shins, as his eyes glinted down at me, all but black in the darkness.

He snarled and spun away, skimming a hand over his close-cut hair.

"You can't go in there," he said, shaking his head. "We compromise. I'll walk you around the block, you go into the coffee shop. I come back here, I'll have my phone on speaker, talk as I do a walk through."

I just stared at him. "What about calling this in or whatever it's called? Aren't you supposed to do that?"

"And what if there's nothing to call in?" He shook his head. "If the house is empty, then what?"

"It won't be empty."

His stark expression didn't soften. "If I find something, then I call. But if you try to go in there, I will haul you away from here over my shoulder, fuck everything else."

I ordered a latte I didn't want and sat in the back of the all-night coffee shop, watching students plunk away at their papers, listening as a couple talk about how expensive the houses were and why it was so insane trying to find a decent house here. *Yeah, guys, it's the Carolina shore. Deal with it.*

My phone rang.

It was Jenks.

"Hello," I said, heart pounding. Everything had better be okay—

Jenks spoke a moment later and my skin broke out into goose bumps.

"I got your email. I'm going to talk to you now because I know you won't hang up. I wasn't using *you*. Yes, I wanted something, but it had to do with your fuck of an ex, not you."

My heart hammered against my ribs.

"You were the last person I planned on coming in contact with, because I thought I knew everything I needed to know about your...type." He paused, sighed. "Call that narrow-minded. I'm sorry. I've known too many women who were abused. It comes with the job. They always go back.

They blame themselves, they blame their parents, they blame everybody but the one person who needs to be blamed—the fucker who did it. Even though I feel all the sympathy in the world for a battered woman, that's not who I saw myself falling for."

I closed my eyes. A battered woman. Not the picture I saw of myself. That wasn't who I wanted to be. Not *who* I saw myself.

"And that's not who you were, either. I was watching you, yeah. But I was watching you hoping he'd show up. He never did and the longer I watched *you*, the harder it got to look away. But I never set out to hurt you. Believe it if you can, if you choose. But I am sorry."

I heard something click. Or maybe it was a snap, like the sound my heart might have made.

"Are you there?" he asked.

"Where else would I be?" I sighed, feeling exhausted. He was right. I wouldn't hang up. I wished I could, though.

"I'm here. Inside Seth's."

I suppose it could have been the door shutting.

"His door wasn't locked. Barely even shut all the way," he said, his voice a bare murmur. Then, louder, he called out, "Seth?"

My breath hitched.

Then it stopped.

"Sugar. I have to call the cops now."

"Jenks?"

"Just stay there," he said, his voice low. He tried for that soothing tone, but I couldn't handle being soothed.

Shoving back, I demanded, "What's wrong?"

A dozen people were staring at me.

I didn't care. Clutching the phone, my heart racing. I demanded again, "Jenks, what is wrong?"

"Just wait there, baby. I'll come to you, soon as I can."

I hung up and started to run.

CHAPTER SEVENTEEN

An ambulance came screaming around the street about the same time I hit the front porch.

The lights were on and that made it that much easier to see Seth.

All the blood.

All the bruises.

He'd fought. And he would have fought hard.

Jenks looked up at me and swore, long and low and I saw the gun in his hand as I came to a sliding halt on my knees next to him.

"He's not dead," I said, the words bubbling out of me. "Tell me he's not, tell me he's not."

"He's not." Jenks turned to me, reached up, his hands coming up to cup my face and I felt the cool, hard surface of the gun pressed against my cheek as he forced me to meet his eyes. "Listen to me, he's not dead, but he's hurt and we have to get him help."

Gulping in a breath of air, I forced myself to stop. Forced myself to breathe.

Not dead.

Seth wasn't dead. "Okay." I nodded. "Okay."

Jenks let me go as a soft, broken moan escaped Seth.

I went to him, going to my knees. "Seth."

He didn't answer.

"Listen to me, Seth," I said. "You can't let him win. You hang on for me. Okay?"

There was no answer and then there was no time for one because there was commotion at the door.

Officers came.
Men in suits.
Paramedics.
I heard Jenks talking in low, hushed voices and then one of the men in a suit approached me.
"You had contact with somebody about this."
My head was spinning.
Seth was hurt.
I didn't know what was going on.
Stiltedly, I told the man in the suit—Captain James Brooks. So innocuous, I thought. Such an innocuous name—the short version about my ex, the vandalism at my house, but he lifted a hand. "I'm familiar with that. I want to know about tonight."
I told him and he looked away, staring at the wall for a long moment and then looking at Jenks.
Jenks stared at him impassively.
A hundred unspoken things seemed to pass between them.
Neither of them looked at me and I wanted to scream. All I really wanted were some simple answers and nobody would give me that. Nobody.
"I understand you were going to meet a friend…Tony?"
I nodded slowly.
"This would be easier if you would talk to me," Brooks said gently. "I want to help. I want to know what's going on and I want to help. But you need to talk to us."
I shuddered out a breath and glanced at Jenks. He had a grim look on his face, but he looked at me and gave a short nod. "He's a good cop, Shadow. Assuming you want to hear anything I have to say."
I wasn't sure if I did or not, but I wanted to help Marla.
So I told Captain James Brooks.
Everything, or as much as I thought he needed to know so he could help Marla.
When I finished, he took me through it again, asking short, concise questions.
I got two texts from Tony, asking if we were still on. I guess that meant Stefan didn't have people watching this place.
I gave the phone to Brooks, let him read each message and eventually, he told me he'd have to take the phone.

"Okay. I think it's safe to assume your friend Marla is in danger?"

"You think?" The words flew out of me, a biting slash of sarcasm that caught me off guard.

From the corner of my eye, I saw Jenks smile, a slash of white teeth in his dark face.

"That might have been a…facetious comment," Brooks said, inclining his head. He stroked his chin. "Would this Tony be helping your ex if he knew that Seth had been hurt?"

"No." I shook my head, certain of that much. "He's a self-centered piece of work, but he loved Seth."

"Okay. Okay." Brooks continued to rub his chin, then he pinned a hard look on me. "If we put you out front, with officers in the house, in the houses across the street and on the perimeter and Lieutenant Jenkins nearby, would you be comfortable talking to this Tony to see what is going on?"

Lieutenant Jenkins?

As he opened his mouth to respond, the captain cut him off.

"Be quiet." Brooks shot him a dark look. "This is already more of a mess than I can even comprehend and we have a woman missing. Whether it's tied to her ex and your sister, I don't know, but we might only have this one shot and we have less than an hour. So shut it."

Sister.

Jenks' gaze came to me then. And in the back of his gaze I saw something. Some that maybe I should have recognized. A haunted look. I knew that look. I saw it every day in my own eyes.

"Sister," I murmured.

He closed his eyes, lowered his head.

Brooks looked between us, a troubled expression on his face.

Silence, taut and strained passed. I broke it, unable to handle it another second. "I'll wait for Tony." Then I said softly, "Although I don't know if anything will happen." Although Tony had called, I still found it hard to believe Stefan wasn't aware of what was going on here, hard to believe he didn't know the cops were here.

He probably knew.

But for Marla's sake, I hoped not.

They took my room key. One of the cops was going to retrieve my MacBook. They needed to start tracking the information on that picture of Marla. I hoped it wasn't too late.

There was no information from Seth.

He had been unconscious when they took him away.

I'd held his hand for one brief second. I wanted to tell him that we'd find Marla, bring her back. But I couldn't make promises without knowing if I could keep them.

The only one I could make was that I'd try to stop my ex-husband this time.

Somehow.

Some way.

I had a wire running down between my breasts.

Sweat trickled down my spine. It was dark and I was supposed to be outside, walking around. That alone almost froze me, but every time the blackness tried to close up around me, I made myself think about Marla.

Nearly thirty minutes before Tony was to arrive, I slid out through the back. I was going to pretend as if I was walking up the street. Somebody would let me know if he was seen on the street any sooner. So far, he hadn't been. One of the cops had checked my home and nobody had been in or out. My alarm system had been reset and now I got notifications even if the door just opened.

Nobody was staying there to watch me.

The knowledge didn't offer me comfort.

I wasn't sure if anything could offer comfort right now.

Marla. Did he have Marla?

I knew how cruel he could be, how vicious his hands, and how strong he was, how he could crush you into the floor, rob you of breath, even the will to live, all while he laughed about it.

I didn't want my friend to have to go through that.

"He's walking up the street toward your friend's house. Looks nervous."

Jenks' voice was a low, steady murmur in my ear.

I practically came out of my skin.

Tony. They had seen Tony. And Tony was nervous?

I was nervous.

"What do I do now?" I asked, staring at nothing. I had a bottle of water, but I thought if I drank any of it, I'd get sick.

It seemed as though a million eyes rested on me and everybody knew what I was doing.

"Just keep on walking down the street." Jenks paused, and in the background I heard voices. He came back to me and said, "We don't want him in their place. If he had anything to do with it, that will alert him that something is off, assuming he doesn't already know."

Assuming.

If.

I didn't like those words.

But at the same time, I was almost positive that Tony didn't know what had been done to Seth. Maybe he wouldn't care so much about Marla, but he loved Seth. I knew that in my bones.

I continued on down the street, my hands cold as ice and fear pounding through me.

Look on the bright side. The absolute worst things that can happen to me have already happened, and I survived. It's a weird sort of pep talk, but if I could survive what Stefan had done, what could Tony do?

Other than try to turn me back over to Stefan, but Stefan couldn't steal me away this time. Not without people noticing. I'd be missed.

People *knew* what was going on. There were cops watching. Jenks was watching.

Swiping my hands down my jeans, I turned the corner and saw a dark shadow up ahead. Familiar. My shoulders went tight and I picked up my pace. Just as Tony's hand would have closed around the elegant iron-worked doorknob, I caught up to him. "Tony."

He looked at me, his eyes wide and startled.

"You…" He blinked, pasted a fake-happy expression on his face. "You're early."

"Yeah. I knew it would take me a while to get here, so I left early. Didn't take as long as I thought it would." I gave him a half-hearted shrug. "Feel like walking? I'm more tired than I thought and if I sit down, I'm going to crash." Then I nodded toward Marla and Seth's, the ache in my chest tightening. "They're probably asleep. We don't want to wake them."

In the dim light, it was hard to see it. Although I hated the dark, I could see well in it. And I had no problem seeing the tiny lines that formed around his eyes, the way his mouth went tight. They lasted only a minute and then he nodded. "Yeah. Good point. Not everybody loves the night like we do."

Dumb-ass. I hate the night. But I nodded and smiled.

We weren't walking ten minutes when his phone rang.

The short, terse message gave me the chills.

"Yes. I understand. I need…yes, yes. I remember, sir."

He tucked the phone away and I glanced at him. "Really late for calls."

He shrugged. "I know. I do business at all hours, though. You know how it goes with clients."

"Yeah. Glad most of my business is online."

He was quiet a minute. "How is that business going? Get a lot of it?"

"Enough." My spine prickled and I casually put some distance between us.

After a minute, he closed it, just as casually. "Still handling all your own business? Emails and such."

"Yes." I stopped, planting my feet wide apart and then I stared at him.

He looked at me. I saw it there, written on his face. "Tell me you called the cops," he whispered, his voice a plea. There was panic all over his face. But it didn't stop him.

He lunged for me.

I threw myself backward. I hadn't ever wanted to be helpless again. I had taken self-defense classes, but it was so hard to overcome that fear, the panic that takes you over when someone tries to hurt you.

Tony's fingers brushed my arm.

But before he could grab me, he was taken to the ground.

His eyes widened with shock as Jenks hauled him up.

"You…"

Jenks flipped him over, drove his knee against his back.

Tony fought him, but Tony worked retail. He did everything from working in music shops to management and he might be physically fit, but he wasn't up to handling the six-foot-two cop who was muscling him into the dirt.

Less than a minute later, two uniformed cops arrived and he was hand-cuffed and dragged upward, crying.

He stared at me, a plea in his eyes. "You don't understand," he said, eyes wide, horrified. "If I don't take you there, he'll kill Marla and Seth will hate me. I…I had to do it."

Jenks leaned in, his voice low, hard as nails. "Take her *where?*"

When Tony had first met Seth, he'd been living in a converted loft that had been left to him by his grandparents. It was outright gorgeous and he could have sold it and made a pretty penny but he held onto it because his parents had loved it, and I think he liked having a home base. Seth had once told me that Tony liked being in love, but he didn't like being in a committed relationship.

It made sense.

The windows of the converted loft were mostly dark, but as they parked, I could see one light. So faint.

Probably the kitchen. It was tucked in the far corner, if I remembered right. I had only been here once.

My gut was tight and frozen.

Tony sat next to me, sweating bullets.

I had to let him walk me up there.

If he did this, and Stefan grabbed me, I was going to try to run. When he stopped me, I would tell him to let me go.

He wouldn't.

We were talking dangerous, dodgy lines, but once I fought him, it was going to give Jenks, who'd just happened to be around, a chance to hear me.

Once they came in, they'd find Marla.

Tony swore she was there.

So much was riding on his word and he was a cowardly liar.

But I couldn't risk her being hurt and we had no time for anything else.

If he slipped away from us, he'd just go right on hurting people. He'd take another shot at me.

Even the beating that Seth had gotten couldn't be traced back to him. Tony had said he'd paid a couple of men to do that.

We had to trap him here, and now.

The next few minutes passed in a rush of voices, reassurances, Jenks' hand on the back of my neck as we paused in the shadows of the building. He'd arrived five minutes earlier, wearing a cap and a heavy jacket that somehow managed to conceal his build. Now he was moving into the building and then we were following, waiting until he was out of sight.

I was supposed to be crying on Tony's shoulder.

How could I do that?

Cry on the shoulder of a man I'd once thought was just sort of a friend?

I'd never trusted him the way I trusted Marla and Seth, but he'd been there when Seth first came to me. He'd been one of the first people I'd laughed with, smiled with.

And now he was walking me up to the man who'd locked me up for nine months. Beaten me. Raped me.

As he slammed down the grate on the elevator, I turned to look at him. "Do you know what he did to me?" I asked, my voice shaking. It wasn't fear. It was rage.

Tony tensed. In the dull lights, I saw something red creep up his neck. "The cops are here. He won't be able to hurt you."

"He locked me in a basement. A dark hole in the ground, no lights, no nothing, for nine months. The only time I heard anything was when I screamed, or when I spoke to myself. Eventually, I stopped speaking. I even stopped screaming."

He flinched.

The elevator continued its slow, clanking crawl.

"He'd come in, like some sort of boogey man and throw me to the floor, rape me. There was food and water left and if I didn't make it last, I'd starve and go thirsty until he came back. Then he stopped coming back."

"Stop it," Tony said, his voice shaking.

"The tornado that hit Boston three years ago...I was there. In that. That's how I got away. It destroyed the house and I climbed out of the rubble. That is the only reason I got away."

The elevator came to a stop.

He reached out to grab my arm.

I sidestepped and shoved him, watched as he slammed back into the wall. Avoiding him as I stepped out into the hall, I said softly, "I'll let you take me in there. But you won't touch me. And you're wrong about how this will play out. You've already lost it with Seth. He'll never forgive you anyway."

The lights were off when we went in.

Stefan, trying to play with my mind, I had no doubt. But I'd walked through the dark to come here.

Somehow, I'd conquered that fear.

Maybe I should thank him for that.

I let some of the nerves I felt creep into my voice. "Ah, can we turn on the lights?"

A soft chuckle echoed through the room.

"Who is that?" I demanded.

"No-nobody," Tony said, his voice even more nervous than mine.

When a hand caught me, I swung out. The surprise wasn't that I connected. The surprise was how good it felt. "Let me go!" Terror flooded me as Stefan slammed me against the wall.

"Grace. How nice to see you," he whispered against my cheek.

"No." I struggled. "Let me go!"

I put every ounce of terror, fear and rage I had into my voice.

Or I tried.

He clamped his hand over my mouth.

It didn't matter, though.

A fist hit the door.

"Everything okay in there?" a voice called out.

Jenks.

My legs went limp and I might have collapsed, but I couldn't stand the thought of being helpless on the floor while Stefan stood.

"Say you're fine," Stefan snarled in my ear. His fingers bit cruelly into my cheek as he squeezed my face. "You know how it will go if you don't."

But I'd been out of his reach for too long. And I knew better now.

"*Help me!*"

There was a tremendous sound and Stefan flung me to the floor. Something wet and sticky met my palms and I fell, stumbling as I tried to get to my feet. A hand caught my wrist and jerked me down. "Stay down," Tony ordered. His voice was low.

I jerked back, refusing to listen.

The lights came on and I blinked, struggling to adjust to the bright, almost vicious glare.

Stefan stood there, smiling. So handsome, so urbane.

And even with a gun in his hand, he looked as though he expected the entire world to fall at his feet.

Jenks stood in front of him, and he wasn't about to fall.

Stefan cocked his head, frowning. "You..." he murmured. "I know you."

"Do you now." Jenks just stared. "I think you need to put that gun down."

Stefan just smiled. "I think you should have stayed outside, minded your own business. Now you'll just be another missing person. You can thank my wife for that, I'm afraid."

Swallowing, I tried to push to my knees and again, my hands slipped out from under me. Looking down, I saw the puddle of red. Dark, sticky red...a moan slipped out of me as I followed the line of it, flowing from the still, broken body in the middle of the kitchen floor. Marla's face, her eyes sightless, stared in my direction and I wanted to scream, wanted to hit something, break something.

"You son of a bitch," I breathed out.

This time, I managed to clamber upright.

"Shadow," Jenks said softly. "Stay there."

Stay there... *No!* I had to go to her. Each step sent me slipping back to the floor and when I reached the counter, I almost did fall. I clutched at it, clinging to it to keep from going back down in that awful, awful pool of red.

Marla. Dead. Because of him.

"Shadow..." Stefan's lip curled. "You...you were at the restaurant. Are you *fucking* my wife?"

"I'm not your *wife!*" I shouted it and it felt so good to do that. Even as my heart broke and fear ripped through me, shouting those words at him freed something inside me. "I'm not your *wife*, you evil son of a bitch. I left you and you couldn't stop me. You tried but you couldn't."

Stefan's head whipped around, and he stared at me.

I swept out my hand and caught something. I didn't even look to see what it was—a half empty can of beer. Hurling it at him, I had a brief second to enjoy the shock that lit his features.

Then Jenks was moving, taking him down.

The sound of the gun going off echoed so very, very loudly.

CHAPTER EIGHTEEN

The hours that came after that were terribly loud, terribly awful. I, who had chased after sensation and light and touch and sound, would have given almost anything for a bit of peace, a bit of silence.

Marla had been dead for some time before I got there. Nothing I did or said would have kept her alive.

Stefan had likely killed her immediately after that email.

She'd never had a chance.

Neither had Seth.

Oh, Seth was alive. But he'd never be the same after this. I spent a great deal of time in the hospital. They wouldn't let me go in to see him. I wasn't family. He had nobody listed as next of kin, though I knew he did have family. There was a rift between them, caused by the trouble he'd gotten into, and stubbornness, he'd told me, on both sides.

So he was alone in there.

And I was alone here.

Jenks had climbed into one of the cop cars.

There had been a low, furious argument between him and the older cop, his boss, I thought. But in the end, Jenks had climbed into that car and I had the feeling that if he hadn't climbed willingly into the front seat, he might have been handcuffed and thrown into the back.

My clearest memory of all of it was the way Stefan had looked at me as the cops dragged Jenks off him. Bloody and broken, his eyes were still cool as they sought out my face.

I'd stared into the face of a madman.

And he had smiled.

"Enjoy your time away, wife," he murmured as the cops had slapped a pair of handcuffs on him.

He truly believed he could get out of this. While Marla's blood had cooled at his feet, he'd thought he could get away with what he'd done.

There was no reasoning like that of a lunatic.

And he still managed to fill me with fear. It was a fear that followed me, even now.

When my phone rang and I saw a familiar name on the display, I almost didn't answer. My gut was tight and cold and my head throbbed. Blood roared in my ears and the metallic taste of fear in my throat was thick and heavy.

Detective Neely.

Swiping my hands down my skirt, I debated whether I should answer and I waited too long.

It went to voicemail and maybe that was better.

It let me stop and panic, stop and pace, stop and almost puke each time the fear got too strong.

Neely was the cop who'd found me on the road all those years ago.

He was a detective now and he'd heard about what had happened. It was enough, he thought, to re-open my case. But he needed to talk with me.

He left a number.

My hands were aching and I looked down, saw that I had them clenched so tight that my knuckles had gone bloodless.

Neely called me three times over the next week.

Seth's mother called many times. I'd tracked her number down and called. She hadn't been home and I'd had to leave a voicemail. I panicked and handled it badly, said he'd been hurt.

She called back within the hour, her voice tight with fear and I wanted to smack myself.

The sanitized version didn't calm her and the next time I heard from her it was to ask if I had the number for the hospital. There were other calls—could I recommend a hotel near the hospital, did he need clothes…

There were no calls from Jenks.

Not a one.

I went to the cottage and it was shut down tight, as if he'd never even been there.

I called and spoke with Detective Barry, gave her his name, told her what I knew. Asked if she knew where he might be.

And I was told I might need to let things lie for a bit. I didn't understand that.

But it made it easier to know what to do when the day came and Neely called again and told me that they needed me to come back to Boston.

It had been almost three weeks since I'd stared at my ex-husband over a pool of cooling blood while death stained the air.

Boston was the very last place on earth I'd ever wanted to see again.

But it was becoming very painful to stay here as well.

An airport is a terribly lonely place at three a.m.

But I'm used to being alone.

Seth had been out of the hospital for almost two weeks. Last week, his brother came up, along with a brother-in-law, and they packed up his things. He was leaving, moving back to Savannah. He wanted to be near his parents, his sister and their kids for a while. He might stay there, he might not. He didn't know. Losing Marla made him realize he needed to mend the rifts between him and his family and it was time to do that.

I understood.

But I missed him.

He might have come back to see me off if I'd asked him, or maybe he'd text me if I told him what was going on.

They had reopened the case against Stefan and they needed me to come back to Boston. Apparently two acquaintances of his had disappeared. One shortly before he met me, and one from almost ten years ago.

What they expected me to tell them, I didn't know.

Although I could tell them about Keilani.

Jenks' sister.

He hadn't told me about her, but that hadn't stopped me from finding out.

I should talk to the cops, tell them they needed to start looking for evidence to connect Keilani to Stefan.

It was time, though, to face the specters of my past and lay them all to rest.

I was just going for a few days, for now.

Eventually, I might have to go back for a trial.

I wondered what would happened if they found evidence against him back in Boston. They planned to try him for Marla's murder and the assault on Seth.

Three years ago, nobody would say one word against the man. Now, I was flying back to speak with a cop about what Stefan had done to me.

And…I sighed and pulled my iPad out, opened the bookmarks to the website.

She had a pretty face. She was darker than Jenks and they had different last names, but you could see the similarities—in their eyes, the shape of their mouths. Her eyes were just as dark as his, not quite as intense. Her hair was black and razor straight, falling halfway down her back. Her smile managed to be both seductive and sweet, all at once.

The picture was one I'd found on her website.

She was the artist of the picture Jenks had shown me all those months ago.

The art was likely how Stefan had found her. Stefan had always had an eye for talent, and a love for seducing artists. Breaking them.

Her name had been Keilani and she'd disappeared a month before I escaped hell.

She'd met him sometime while he was still married to me. I was left to piece it all together on my own, but I could see how it all happened. She'd moved to Boston the year before I tried to divorce him, had a showing at a smaller gallery. He had bought a few of her pieces and still had them in his gallery—I had seen them when I did a search.

She might have been one of the women he taunted me with. She might have been one of the women I never knew about. She was most certainly one of the women he'd hurt, though.

One of the pictures of her I found online had her wearing a necklace of pink pearls. I'd been forced to wear such a necklace to a gallery showing. And I remembered seeing her. I only remembered her because I'd noticed how beautiful she was, and then I saw the hurt in her eyes, the misery, as she stared at my necklace, then looked at the man behind me.

A part of me had thought, *You can have him.*

I'd worn the necklace only the once, because when we got home, he ripped it off of me after he'd raped me, then he blamed me for being so careless with my lovely new gift.

My belly hurt just thinking of it.

I didn't know what he'd done to her.

But I'd have to tell the police about the necklace.

If I ever saw Jenks again, I'd have to tell him as well.

That moment, though, seemed years away from here and now. In the dark, quiet airport where everybody seemed to exist in a fog. Including me.

My eyes felt gritty and tired but I couldn't sleep. Not here. Not exposed. I'd come to grips with the fact that I would never *be* normal, never feel normal. I might get closer and maybe the dark didn't bother me as much as it once did.

Maybe the day would come and I could face my ex-husband in court, watch as they handed down a sentence and I could know he would be locked away, never able to hurt me again. I could think of it, pray for it.

Maybe after that happened, I could stop being so afraid and I could look at him and tell him that he no longer had the power to hurt me.

But I could never let my guard down the way I might want.

Then again, I didn't know if I really *wanted* to let my guard down. I'd tried. I'd trusted somebody.

I'd had my heart ripped out. I still didn't know why Jenks had ever approached me at all, what he'd wanted. Or why he'd just walked away from me.

It had been weeks and not a word.

The last time I'd tried to call him, I was told the number was disconnected.

It was as if he no longer even existed.

A weary sigh worked its way out of me. Instinctively, I reached for my bag and pulled out a sketchpad. It was a fresh one and I rooted around until I found a pencil. The lines of his face were familiar to me now, as familiar to me as my own. Even as familiar to me as the devil who'd haunted so many nightmares.

And just as real.

As his face came to life before me, I locked on that, focused on it. He was real.

He just didn't want me.

Neely met me at the airport.

He stood there, solid and square, in a suit instead of a uniform and I looked at him, my eyes immediately finding him in the crush.

Neely had a wide, friendly face, the sort of face that made you want to trust him.

He had a partner and he'd told me all about Ginny Chadwick, but she wasn't there with him.

It was just us, and I was glad.

His hands came up, caught mine. I squeezed and tried not to think about how the wind had ripped his voice away and the lightning had cast his face in stark relief that night so long ago.

Three years ago.

A lifetime ago.

Maybe even two lifetimes.

I was no longer the girl who had jumped at every sound and let men spy on her as she walked to the beach three times a week.

I don't know who I am and I don't know how long it will take to figure it out.

But I could let him squeeze my hand and when somebody bumped into me, I didn't jump in fear.

I'm getting there. One day, I might even be whole.

"You look well," Neely said, his voice soft and steady. He didn't even sound surprised as he said it.

With a shrugged, I tugged my hands back and adjusted the strap of my bag. "Some days, I almost even feel well."

"You'll be okay, kid." He looked as though he wanted to say more but, in the end, we just sought out the baggage claim and walked there in silence.

Outside, Boston gleamed beautiful and clear in the fall. There had been a time when I loved Boston in autumn. The crisp, cold air. Now, I was dispassionate and I couldn't think of anything I wanted more than to get on a plane and fly back home to warm beaches and soft sand and sunshine...and Jenks.

Damn him.

"...lunch?"

I looked over at Neely, distracted. "I'm sorry. My mind was wandering."

"It's okay. I was wondering if you'd like to get some lunch. Settle a bit before we have to get to work."

Settle.

Eat.

No.

My bag came down the carousel and I caught it. Neely didn't offer to help and I was glad. I needed to keep my hands busy. Fiddling with the strap, I looked at the rest of the bags on the conveyor belt and then turned, cutting through the people before I stopped and looked back at Neely.

"I want to go there," I said softly.

He didn't pretend not to understand.

Three years had passed.

I didn't know how this place had looked before, but I'd never forget how it looked on that night.

It was nothing like this.

Pretty homes.

Nothing like the elegant, graceful house where I had lived with Stefan, but pretty. The sort of place a young family would want to live. I saw a mom walking with her young son, an older couple walking hand in hand. It seemed an insult that he would bring me here, keep me here, in a place where happy people made homes.

But horror thrives everywhere. I've seen that firsthand.

Neely stopped in front of a house that had vacant windows, pulling the car to the curb and letting the engine idle. "He still owns the house. Had it rebuilt exactly the way it was before it was destroyed in the tornado."

My breath started to come in erratic stops and starts. Fumbling with my seat belt, I finally managed to free it and climbed outside, my legs rubbery, yet stiff at the same time. I could hardly move. Could hardly breathe. The sunshine was warm on my skin, but I was cold to the bone.

"Rebuilt," I said, my lips barely moving. "Exactly."

I stared at it, searching for one of the windows that had let me see the lightning. Lightning that had lit my way to freedom. The storm had sent debris flying and it had busted open the door to the small room in the basement that had been my cell.

Was it still there?

I didn't remember moving, but I must have because Neely's hand caught my wrist and I looked down, dumbstruck at the sight of the rock in my hand.

"Don't," he said, his voice gentle. "I understand the desire, but don't. You got out. That's something that will eat at him for the rest of his life."

"It shouldn't be here," I said, and I had to force each word out, as if dragging them out from the very depths of my broken soul.

"No. It shouldn't." His eyes were flat as he shifted his gaze past me to look at the house. "It should be torn down and the earth salted so nothing ever grows here, nothing ever thrives there. But it's not up to us."

CHAPTER NINETEEN

I would have thought it wouldn't be so hard to be there.

The monster from my nightmares was still in jail back in South Carolina.

The cops were staying in touch. His family had hired a lawyer, a top-notch one, and they'd pushed for him to be released on bail.

The judge hadn't been impressed by the pedigree of a Boston blue-blood. She'd stared at him over the rims of her glasses, smacked down all attempts to argue, and denied any requests for bail.

For now, Stefan was rotting behind bars.

I shouldn't be terrified to be alone in Boston.

But many things *shouldn't* be, yet are.

There I was, huddling in a hotel bed with my blankets drawn up high and my skin chilled, shaking. And I was back to sleeping with the lights on.

Not all of the lights, but one.

The one in the hotel bathroom, just enough shining in on me that I wasn't in total darkness as I slept.

When the knock came, I almost went out of my skin.

I didn't handle surprises well.

Peering through the judas hole, I caught my breath when I saw who it was.

Closing my eyes, I pressed my brow to the door and just stood there. Uncertain what to do, how to react, I just stood there. Waited. After a second, I opened my eyes to stare at him.

Jenks lifted a hand to the door.

"Open up," he said quietly.

I didn't say anything.

"I know you're there, sugar." Wide shoulders rose and fell. "I can feel you there, watching me. Let me in."

Slowly, I reached up and freed the locks.

I opened it and then backed away as he came inside.

His hair had grown out a little and he looked as though he hadn't had much more sleep than I. The hotel room shrank by half as his gaze raked over me.

I had absolutely no idea what to say to him. I had absolutely no idea why he was here.

But as his eyes lingered on my face, none of that really mattered. His gaze dropped to my mouth and heat, hunger rolled through me.

My skin burned and my heart pounded.

One thing I did know.

I still wanted, needed, *craved* him.

I reached for him and his arms closed around me. His mouth opened under mine and for once, something did make sense.

Shoving the jacket off his shoulders, I jerked at his shirt while he fought with the pajamas I'd pulled on hours ago. They had seemed simple and warm and comfortable but now they were itchy and confining and I wanted to be naked, pressed against that long, hard body.

Fabric caught, tore under his hands but I didn't care.

All I cared about was getting his shirt off, then freeing him from his jeans and then I had him in my hands, but it wasn't enough. I went to my knees, stared at him. My breath hitched as I remembered that sketch, the one I'd drawn months ago. Leaning in, I paused as his hands came up, cradling my head. I wanted to see this, see us, but I'd just have to imagine it. I could do that. Wrapping my hand around the base of his cock, I leaned in closer, licked the head of him, heard him groan.

A rush of warmth and heat gathered between my thighs.

I took him into my mouth and sucked him deep. He rocked against me and I moved on him faster and faster, wanting to feel him come in my mouth. His cock jerked, almost viciously, and then I was on my feet, in his arms.

"No. Like this," he muttered against my neck as he urged me to the wall and caught me up, pressing between my thighs.

I looked, watching as he pressed against me. Swollen and hard, still wet from my mouth…wet from me now, too, as he rubbed the head back and forth against my folds. "Take me in, Shadow," he whispered.

I arched my back, my breath catching as he slid in.

We both watched, our gazes locked on the slow, intimate possession, his cock sinking into me, my flesh wet and swollen, stretched tight around him. A whimper escaped me and he grunted out my name as he seated himself completely inside. "There..." he muttered. "Just there. Fuck, I missed this. Missed you."

My gaze shot to his.

He looked right back, lifting his hand to my face. "I told you once..." he rasped. "This is where I want to be."

And then he set about proving it, fucking me slow and steady, and even when I tried to urge him, he didn't let me. It was a careful claiming and I had no doubt he was intent on making sure I knew one thing—he did want me.

The question was...

Why?

With him there, I was able to turn the light off.

Wrapped in his arms, I could feel myself sliding closer to sleep but I wasn't so ready to give in yet.

Muscles limp, body sated, I forced my brain to stay awake.

He never had answered me. I understood more, now. But it was because I'd chased those answers.

Not because he'd given them to me.

It mattered, too. That he give them to me, that he trusted me enough. That he let me trust him.

"Why are you here?" I asked him softly.

He had one hand curved over my hip. His other arm was under my head. His mouth pressed to my shoulder. "I'm here for the same reason I've always been here," he murmured. "I can't stay away. Even when I know I should." He pressed closer, his voice low and raw, a mutter against my skin, a song against my soul. "You're in my blood, in my heart, in my soul, and I can't cut you out."

The words throbbed inside me, pulsed.

They meant something, more than just pretty words and I wanted to hold them tightly and cling to them, but I needed more, still. Closing my hand around his, I squeezed my eyes shut and searched inside for the courage. "I..."

He rubbed his cheek against my shoulder, a silent encouragement for whatever I had to say.

Slowly, I sat up. I had to be away from him when I said this because if I wasn't, it would make it too easy to just forget. To fall back against him and let him do…whatever. Be whatever. Forget the hurt of the past month, forget the confusion. Just exist.

I'd existed for a long while and it had led me to him. Was it really a bad thing?

My eyes flew open while the answer pulsed and beat inside me.

Yes.

I didn't want to *exist*.

I wanted to live and I couldn't do this with whatever shadow lay between us.

"I want to know about your sister."

The change in him was instantaneous.

He pulled away and I felt chilled at the distance. Chilled at the loss of *him*.

Turning, I saw him staring at the wall, sitting on the far edge of the bed. His head bowed and those wide shoulders rose and fell on a sigh. "We don't need to talk about her, sugar."

"Don't we?"

In a violent surge of movement, he came up off the bed and started to pace. The hotel room had never seemed smaller, those long legs of his eating up the space with angry, quick strides. He came to the window and stopped there, staring out, uncaring of the fact that he stood there, naked and beautiful, all golden skin and muscles and power.

"What is there to talk about?" Jenks asked, his voice weary. "She's gone. She disappeared just over three years ago."

Three years ago. I shivered, thinking back to what had happened to *me* during that time period.

"She was last seen leaving a club in Boston. Reports are conflicted— some say she was with a short white guy, others say a tall black guy, others say she was alone. One thing *everybody* will agree to—she wasn't seen with anybody that even resembles Stefan fucking Stockman."

He stood there, relaxing against the window, and all that edgy, massive temper had disappeared, sucked inside him as if it had never existed. His voice was soft, almost lazy.

It was, I thought, completely terrifying.

Especially when he turned and looked me. When I saw the hell in his eyes. When I saw the fury.

"I knew she was seeing him," he said, his voice still soft. Still level. "Keilani told me. Didn't tell anybody else and I didn't know up until three weeks before she disappeared. I knew there was somebody. Lani had a thing for guys who were just no good for her and I was already making plans to come out here, see what she was up to. I could tell by her conversations with Mom, the way she was online, her Facebook page, that she was caught up in somebody again. It went on for months and I'd call, try to get her to talk. And…nothing. Then she calls me one night, tells me that there's this guy. She loves him." He laughed, and the sound was raw. So raw and ugly. "Tells me his first name and how she thinks there's never been a guy who could make her feel that way. My gut is already crawling and I push for more but she won't tell me. She hangs up and I start digging. Find out there's a Stefan at one of the galleries where she works. I put two and two together and figure out it's him. Not that anybody can help me pin anything down. They were never even *seen* together."

"He was always careful," I said when he fell silent, turning his head to look out the window. Unwittingly, my hand went to my arm, rubbed it. I could remember a hundred times when he'd left me all but ready to beg for the end. But when morning came, there wasn't even a bruise. If he was that careful with me, he'd be just as careful with everything else, especially anything that had to do with his public image. He had always been rather particular about that.

Jenks didn't even seem to realize I'd spoken. "The last time I talked to her was the day before she disappeared. I was booking a plane to come out here. I knew something was wrong. She'd called, crying. Wouldn't tell me what was going on, but something damn well *was* wrong. I tried like hell to get her to talk to me, but she just wouldn't." His lids drooped low, shielding his eyes. "Her best friend was trying to call me while I was in the air. I touched down and there were a dozen emails. They'd been trying to get hold of her since the night before. She hadn't shown up at work. Wouldn't answer email, her phone. She just vanished."

He looked at me.

I knotted my hand in the sheet, unable to speak or think.

"I took a few days leave, stayed while the cops opened the case. But then the storm hit…" He rubbed his face. "You got any idea what it's like trying to solve a missing person's case in the middle of a natural disaster? Lani more or less got pushed to the back burner. She was young, flighty… had skipped out on her rent twice and although there weren't any money issues at the time, they all assumed that was what she was doing. Her apartment showed no signs of a struggle and she hadn't reported anything weird."

"They let it go."

He shifted his eyes to me. "They completely let it go. And my baby sister was just gone."

"What did *you* do?" I stared at him. The man in front of me wasn't the kind of man who'd just let something like that slide by. He'd drag the answer out of the earth's bedrock if he had to.

For the longest time, he just stood there, staring at nothing.

Then he shifted his attention to me. "I was in the hospital, one day. Where you were."

I tensed.

My hands curled into the sheets and my heart started to race while my gut twisted in a vicious fury.

"I thought maybe I could talk to you, see if you knew anything." His gaze locked on mine.

All I wanted to do was look away.

And it was the last thing I *could* do.

"But then somebody went in there, while I was still trying to figure out the right way to talk to you." He skimmed a hand back over his hair, turned back to the window. "It was the rape advocate. I moved closer, started to listen. You told her you didn't want to talk. You had just spent too much time in hell and you weren't ready to go back there, not for anything." His jaw clenched and I watched as a muscle pulsed, twitched there. "She kept trying to get you to talk and I just wanted to tell her to shut the fuck up and leave you alone. After about five minutes, *you* did that and she left."

My breath hitched and I was finally able to look away. "You had no right," I said, squeezing the words out through my tight throat.

"No. I didn't. And I'm sorry." A dull red flush crawled up his neck. "I did more than that, though. Because if I thought you might know about Lani, I would have talked to you. I didn't want to put you through anything but if she…" He stopped, shook his head. "I had to know. I followed the counselor to the elevator, bumped into her. She was making all these little notes and I swiped her notebook."

Unable to breath, I shot up off the bed and half-stumbled, half-ran into the bathroom, wrapped in the sheet.

It took ten minutes of splashing my face with cold water before I could come back out. I'd left the sheet in the bathroom and pulled on my robe. Jenks had pulled his jeans on at some point, but he was in his spot, staring out into the night.

"You son of a bitch."

The only sign I had that he heard me was the way his shoulders tightened oh so minutely.

"You *son of a bitch!*"

I grabbed my shoe from the floor and hurled it at him. It hit the back of his head.

Slowly, he turned around and his face could have been carved from stone. "I'm sorry," he said, the words curt and harsh.

"You think that's good enough?"

"No." He inclined his head. "But that's all I got. And I will tell you now, if I had to make the choice, I'd do it all over again. Once I read what had happened, I knew you didn't know anything so I moved on, tried other avenues."

"You *moved on?*" I gaped at him.

"What was I supposed to do?" He crossed the distance between us, staring down at me. "Especially after I read what he'd done to *you*. He could have my sister out there somewhere. I had no idea where she was, what he could have done to her. I wasn't just going to let her be abandoned like that."

I hated that he made sense. I hated that those words managed to trickle through the veil of fury that held me. I hated that I *understood*.

Turning away from him, I moved over to the suitcase I had yet to fully unpack. One of the thousand little rebellions I'd continued throughout my life. Everything had its place—and naturally, I refused to put anything in its place unless I had to. Digging through the jumble of clothes, I found a T-shirt and jeans. Without looking at him, I pulled them on, painfully aware that I was naked beneath them, but I needed more than just a robe to face him now and I couldn't take the time to find anything more than that.

"So you've spent the past three years looking for her."

Silence was the only answer.

Pulling my hair out from under my collar, I turned to look at him.

He had gone gray. Gray. And it was as if he'd aged ten years since he'd climbed from my bed. "No." He shook his head. "No."

His hands were trembling.

I felt sick as I saw that fine tremor. He pulled his wallet out, pulled out a neat square of newspaper—folded up and tucked inside the compartment where he keep his cash.

He held it out to me and turned away.

Dismembered human remains found beneath the floor of building set to be demolished

My belly felt hot, tight and greasy.

Blood roared in my ears, pounded.

My eyes were tight and dry.

Instinctively, I bent over and breathed shallowly, waited for the black dots crowding my vision to pass and then I started to read, skimming everything but the important bits and pieces.

My lip curled instinctively as I saw the area.

I knew it. Province. Not too far from Cape Cod. Stefan's family owned land there and we'd spent time there each summer. I hated it, but it was part of being a Stockman, so it had been my life.

The building has sat vacant for years....

...freshly poured concrete...

...steel drum...

My vision fuzzed out on me, briefly, as I read about the grizzly contents. Human hands.

He'd taken her hands.

The cruelest thing you could do to an artist.

"You're certain it's her?"

"She had a tattoo. A dolphin that wound around her thumb." He took the clipping, folded it up, tucked it back into his wallet. "I'm sorry. And I know it's not enough because I'd do it again if I thought it would help me save her."

I didn't know what to do.

I didn't know how to answer that.

My legs felt awkward and stiff, but I couldn't stay where I was.

When I wrapped my arms around him, for the longest time he didn't touch me back.

When he did, it was to clamp me against him.

We stayed like that for a very long time.

Dawn found me awake.

I hadn't slept since he'd told me the truth.

Everything inside me was a jumble.

I understood what he had done.

Maybe not from his viewpoint, but I could understand it from mine. If I had a brother, a cousin, a father, anybody who could have saved me from Stefan, I hoped they would have done it.

Jenks had tried to do just that.

I could understand.

But in my gut, I knew he wasn't done.

Staring out into the coming morning, I pressed one hand against the glass and tried to still the ache in my chest.

Sometime soon, I might have the chance to face my demon, once and for all.

And then, I would walk away from him.

Once and for all.

I'd claim all those broken and ragged pieces he'd taken and I'd find a way to make them fit.

If Jenks continued to chase after this, I wasn't going to have the peace I needed.

Maybe it was selfish of me.

I don't know.

And I realized I couldn't let it matter.

Not now.

Not anymore.

They had taken too much. Not just Stefan, although he'd stolen damn near everything. It had started with the death of my parents, continued with my aunt's careless guardianship and gone on for years.

It was time to make myself matter.

And if I didn't put myself first, now, it wasn't ever going to happen.

If he chased after the answers to his sister's disappearance, I wasn't going to be first to him.

I would probably never be first.

Where had he been the past month?

Had he called?

Had he made sure I was okay?

A soft, low sigh came from behind me and I tensed in the moments before he touched my back.

"You think heavy thoughts," he murmured.

The bed shifted as he moved around and sat up behind me. He pulled me against him and I let him, sank against him and enjoyed the sensation of it, his chest against my back, his skin hot against my own, his body so strong and steady.

I'd miss this, more than I could probably imagine.

"What are you going to do now?" I asked him.

"What do you mean?"

Staring down, I focused on my hands, the way they looked at they covered his. Mental snapshot, so I could draw this. Absently, I glanced up and realized I could see the mirror, the way we looked together in the coming light. Another sketch to draw. Another memory.

"You found me on the beach for a reason. You never did tell me what it was."

His arms tensed slightly. "I didn't *find* you. I live there...not on the beach. That was my parents' cottage. They left it to us, but Lani liked it more so she was there more than I was. I was out there six months ago. It was her birthday…and I saw you. Recognized you from the start."

The knot around my heart eased a little. It never occurred to me that he might lie.

That it was an accident, how he'd come into my life this time made it easier.

"And?"

He turned his face into my neck. "And…I don't know. I watched you. Followed you to your house once…and I saw the guy across the street. So I decided I'd go back. And he was there. Again. I got his name, tracked him to your husband. Figured I'd keep an eye on you. Then it got to be more than that."

He fell silent and I had nothing to say to break that silence. It was awkward and weird and deep inside, my heart was like a stone in my chest.

"Weeks went by," he finally murmured. "I told myself I needed to approach you. Then I'd tell myself maybe that fucker was going to show up and I could make my move then. I was torn between an obsession with you…and my hate for him. It froze me. Then you left that sketchbook on the beach."

Blood climbed up my neck. "You must have thought I was pathetic."

With a hand tangled in my hair, he tugged on my head until our eyes met. "No. I thought a lot of things, but that one never entered my mind. And that obsession just got worse. You're inside me, Shadow. In so many ways. I…"

His gaze held mine.

I thought maybe I saw what he wanted to say.

Before he could, I lifted a hand, touched his lips.

I couldn't hear it now.

Slipping from the bed, I moved to the window and looked outside. In three hours, I had to be at the police station, had to talk to Neely, the detectives who'd handled my case all those years ago. Who knew how many times I'd have to go over this?

"Are you going to try to get them to reopen her case?" I asked.

"It's now or never."

I nodded. Yes. Now or never.

Looking back at him, I clenched my hands into fists, so tightly my nails bit into my skin.

"Until you came into my life, I was only a shadow," I said softly. "That's all I was. I used to think about the time when Stefan had me—both the marriage and the months he held me trapped—as some sort of bad movie, or a nightmare. If it wasn't real, it was easier to think about. It's a little easier, *now*, to think about it. Which is good, because it's time to face it. Face it, then put it behind me."

Jenks watched me, his gaze so focused, so intense. I couldn't blink without him noticing.

"I have to do this," I said, forcing myself to open one hand as it started to ache. "It's going to be hell, and I have to do it anyway."

Jenks came off the bed, came to a stop in front of me. He reached up, cupped my cheek. "I'll be there with you."

My heart shattered. Closing my hand around his wrist, I tugged it away. "You can't."

Confusion lit his eyes.

Turning away, I stared at the glass. I saw nothing beyond it. The tears blinded me now. "I need somebody who can give me everything," I said, my voice shaking. "And half of you is going to be focused on what happened to your sister. It's not fair to you if I make you choose."

Because I was trying not to be a coward, I made myself look at him as I said, "But it's not fair to me if I have to settle for any less."

Jenks had gone rigid, his eyes black in his face. "Shadow?"

"If you do this, he's going to be between us. He'll be a shadow in our lives until you find answers. And if you never find them, then I settle for nothing." I blinked until my vision cleared, forced myself to breathe. "He made me nothing once already. He stripped me down to nothing, until there was no light, no sound, no voice, no hope. I deserve to be somebody's everything. I can't be that if you spend half your life chasing after revenge."

"You think I don't need to find answers?" he rasped.

Lifting a hand, I touched it to his heart. "No. You need those answers. And if you ever find them, I'll be waiting." Then I turned away.

I didn't make it two feet before he caught me, caging me by the small table, his mouth to my ear, his long, powerful body shaking. "Don't do this, Shadow." His voice was a desperate plea in my ear. I wanted so badly to listen. I wanted so badly to give him everything.

"I don't have a choice."

CHAPTER TWENTY

"**H**e says he'll take a plea bargain."

I stared at Neely, at Detective Barry, then looked at the lawyers, my heart slamming away in shock.

It had been more than a year since that awful night in Tony's apartment and each day I expected to wake up and find out that it had all been a horrid, awful joke.

That Stefan was still out there, that he would still come for me.

Or worse, that the jury would mess it up and he'd walk.

A plea bargain.

This was... I couldn't understand it.

Beneath the table, I laced my hands together. My chest ached and I realized I hadn't taken a breath. Forcing myself to do just that, I waited until the ache subsided and then looked at the lawyer.

"A plea bargain."

"Yes. We're looking at twenty years in jail, although..." Quincy Kestler pursed his lips, frowned as he shuffled the papers. Then he set them down and looked at me. "Well, it's complicated. He'll do his twenty years here. Whether he does any time in Massachusetts depends on what happens there. But there's a stipulation. He wants to talk to you."

My mouth went dry.

My heart knocked against my ribs.

For one painful minute, I couldn't breathe at all.

Twenty years.

That was a very, very long time.

It wasn't long enough.

"What about the cases in Massachusetts?"

"There's nothing to stop us from trying him." Neely shrugged. "And we've got a lot of time to look for evidence."

Twenty years was a lot of time for evidence to disappear.

"How long do I have to talk to him?"

Neely watched him with understanding eyes. "That's completely up to you, I'd think."

Quincy leaned in, folded his hands. "The bottom line is, things don't look good for him. He relied on his family and his money too long. People here aren't as impressed with the Boston bluebloods. Money is fine, but power matters more and he just doesn't impress people as much in this state as he thinks. There's too much evidence against him and he knows it. You give him a few minutes, he agrees to the deal and we'll tell him you can give him a few more after it's all said and done. Might be the best way to do it. If he waives his right to appeal, then it's all over for him."

And maybe, I thought, for me, too.

Maybe.

It was that thought that had guided me to this.

Stefan smiled like a shark as he accepted the deal, smiled at me as I sat in front of him.

And I stared at him, wished I could smile back at him. Wished I could find some way to act as though I wasn't terrified. It was more than I could manage, but at least I held his eyes as he looked me over. His gaze lingered on my hair. My heart jumped into my throat and I had a flash of what had happened once when I'd styled it in a way he hated. He'd shoved my head into a tub of water, scrubbing the gel and hairspray out while I choked and almost drowned.

Today my hair was colored through with streaks of gold and green and blue and red. All the colors of the rainbow. And it was the shortest I'd ever gone, even shorter than the choppy chin-length bob I'd had when I'd first met Jenks.

Defiantly, I arched a brow and stared him down.

A slow smile curled his lips.

"You look lovely, Grace."

Slumping in the chair, I folded my arms over my chest, stared at the window. I wouldn't answer to that name.

"Aren't you going to talk to me?"

Shifting my gaze to him, I said, "That's not my name."

"If you want me to sign that plea agreement, your name is whatever the fuck I choose it to be."

My belly went tight and queasy and the response trembled on my lips, even as I almost looked away, out of deference, just the way he'd always wanted.

Instead, I shoved back, the legs of my chair scraping over the floor. "I'm done here." I looked at Quincy, saw the way his mouth tightened. "If he wants a puppy to jump through hoops, you found the wrong woman."

I wasn't even three feet away when he started to laugh.

"Well, well, well. You went and grew claws. And there's even the hint of a spine."

Stopping in my tracks, I looked back at him. "I had enough of a spine to leave you," I said. My voice shook, but I managed to hold his gaze and glare at him.

"And look how far you made it." He tapped his nails on the table. "Do you dream of that little hole, my dear? Do you dream of the nights I came to you?"

"Do you?"

"Oh, yes." He studied me, still smiling. Then he gestured for his lawyer. "I'm told you'll come back to see me, if I go through with the agreement. I have conditions."

Why wasn't I surprised?

"One visit a month, for the length of my incarceration." He gifted me with a smile. "I'll take your word that you'll hold your end of the bargain."

I curled my lip at him. "Not on your life."

"Then I won't sign. I'll get off and I'll come after you."

"Good luck."

I made it to the door this time.

"One year."

I paused. Looked up and saw Neely watching me. I could feel Quincy's eyes on me as well.

My heart slammed against my ribs and I closed my eyes, pressed my forehead to the door. "I have a condition of my own."

"Oh?"

Slowly, I turned and faced him.

"Do tell." He looked like a giant cat, playing with its mouse.

"You had a lover. Keilani. An artist." I managed to actually smile this time, although it was tight and strained and I thought my face might crack. "She disappeared about the time you and I...had our falling out. I want to know more about her."

His eyes narrowed. "What makes you think I know anything?"

"Call it instinct."

"And what do you want to know?"

"Everything." My gut twisted into snarls.

He rubbed his fingers together. "I'll tell you. A little each visit."

"Done." I walked forward and rested my hands on the table, staring him down. "But the day you stop talking, that's the day I stop coming to see you. Are we in agreement?"

"Of course." His smile was slow. Reptilian.

I turned and walked slowly out, the cops at my back.

My knees were shaking. But I didn't collapse until I was out of Stefan's sight.

Almost ten years ago on this day, I met the man who would become my husband, my tormenter, my rapist, my would-be killer.

Now, I sat in the courtroom in Charleston, South Carolina and watched as the judge spoke to him.

My hands were icy cold and my stomach was twisted into snarls.

His parents weren't there.

They'd washed their hands of him once they'd learned he was signing a deal.

It was one thing to rigorously defend your son.

It was another thing to learn he'd signed a deal admitting guilt.

They'd find a way to weather this travesty.

They were the Stockmans. They always came out smelling like roses.

Stefan was dressed in an elegant suit, Italian, I'd bet, and he looked cool and unperturbed, as though he wasn't facing twenty years in jail.

As the judge finished, he turned to look at me. Then he smiled and handed the woman at his left a letter, nodded in my direction.

I didn't want to see it. Didn't want to read it.

I had a feeling I'd do it anyway, because my mind wouldn't let me rest otherwise. That was the hold he still had on me.

It was with little fanfare as he was led away.

I left the courtroom and she found me, pushed the letter into my hands while hate shone from her eyes. One of the many he'd blinded.

Part of me wanted to tell her that she should thank me. She had no idea the hell I'd saved her from.

And it didn't matter. She wouldn't care, because she couldn't see.

Neely spoke to me. Barry spoke to me. So many people spoke to me and I couldn't hear a word.

Their voices were too loud and jarring and I wanted peace. Just plain and simple peace. A quiet beach.

And—

A hand touched my arm.

Time fell away as I looked up, met Jenks' eyes.

Still clutching that letter, I sucked in a breath.

And when he asked me if I wanted to grab some coffee, all I could do was nod dumbly.

"I had to see."

I nodded. I understood.

"It doesn't feel real," I said, my voice thick.

The letter was a crumpled mess in my lap. I needed to read it but I had no interest in doing it yet.

All I wanted to do was stare at Jenks.

He looked tired.

He looked beautiful.

I wanted to crawl across the table, press myself against him and find that one, last missing piece of me. It was him. It had been him all this time, but I could live without that one piece and until he was ready to be whole as well, I wasn't going to exist in limbo.

He reached out, caught some of my hair, tugged. "This is different."

"Yeah." I shrugged self-consciously. "He had a thing for my hair. Long, straight. If I was attending a business function, it should be worn in a French twist. If I was working out, a bun or a ponytail was acceptable. Any other time, I wore it straight. That was how it was. Now…it's not."

Jenks watched me for a moment. "So if one of these days, you show up with your hair shaved off, will you feel better?"

I laughed. "No. I won't go that far. But this…" I toyed with one of the pink strands. "It fits. And I like it."

"So do I." He watched me. "I miss you. It's like I'm missing a piece of me."

Tears threatened. "I…yeah. I understand that."

He nodded, looked away. Then he slid out from behind the table, came around, pressed his lips to my cheek. "One of these days, I'll get to where the answers aren't as important," he promised. The touch of his lips was a hot little thrill against my skin.

He straightened up, watched me for a long moment. Then he put a card down on the table.

No, I thought, as he walked away. He wasn't going to reach that point. But it didn't matter.

I had the means to get the answers for him.

Or at least a start. He was a good cop, I'd bet. All I had to do was get him the right starting point and he could figure it out. I reached for the card, saw that it had his name, a phone number.

Private investigator.

He'd walked away from the badge.

Maybe it was easier to chase those answers if he didn't watch those lines so closely.

I waited until that night to read the letter.

I probably should have burned it.

Grace,

I imagine you think you're safe now. Tucked up inside your safe little house, in your safe little bed, with the doors locked. I often smile as I think of how you pace the floors, checking each lock, once, twice, three times.

Check them, dear one. Don't think you can stop because I am locked up.

It isn't enough, you see.

I wasn't the only one who came into that basement.

You think I was the only one who played with you? Toyed with you?

I flung it down.

The scream rose in my throat.

Lies, I thought to myself. Desperate to believe just that. It was nothing but lies. And I had to believe it.

Had to.

Scrambling out of bed, I started for the door, ready to check the locks. I'd gotten better about it. I hadn't done it in nearly a week, once I realized he wasn't going to be out on the street. And even before that, I sometimes managed to check the locks only once.

Sometimes.

I stopped before I left my room.

No.

I wasn't going to do this.

He did it only because he'd lost the ability to control me after they slammed the door shut behind him.

He couldn't contact me in anyway, couldn't attempt to have me watched or followed—not that I believed it would fully stop him.

Stefan would be more careful, I had no doubt of that.

But I was safe, inside my home.

And when I walked into that jail next month, I was going to be able to look at him and tell him that he'd failed.

Instead of checking the locks, I went to the shower.

I scrubbed myself, using an entire bar of soap. I washed my hair, three times over.

It was nearly two a.m. when I returned to bed. I didn't even think about what I was doing when I reached for the phone.

Yes, he still needed answers.

But just then, I needed him.

Everything else could wait.

He rang the doorbell less than an hour later.

I threw myself against him and clung to him, almost desperate.

For a little while, I felt whole.

It was enough.

For now.

www.shilohwalker.com

LOOK FOR SHILOH'S LATEST...

Ruined

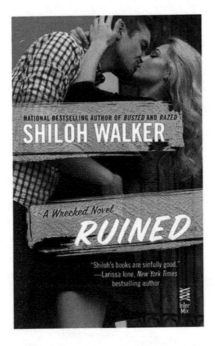

One of the Barnes brothers, Sebastien has always felt blessed. Not only does he have an amazing family, but he's become a Hollywood golden boy who has everything he's ever wanted—with one exception. He's had a thing for Marin since he was a kid, but when he finally summons the courage to ask her out, she turns him down. Marin is ready to settle down, she wants commitment and stability, and Sebastien is still too much of a playboy, caught up in the wild life of the spotlight.

Still reeling from the rejection, Sebastien's luck runs out later that night when he saves a girl from an assault. The shining knight role fits him just fine, but his armor—and his perfect life—become tarnished when the near-deadly attack lands him in the hospital. Physically scarred, he gives up acting and retreats from everybody.

If anyone can pull Sebastien back from the abyss, it's Marin. But first she has to convince him that beauty is *not* only skin deep...

www.shilohwalker.com

ABOUT THE AUTHOR

Shiloh Walker has been writing since she was a kid. She fell in love with vampires with the book Bunnicula and has worked her way up to the more…ah…serious works of fiction. Once upon a time she worked as a nurse, but now she writes full time and lives with her family in the Midwest. She writes romantic suspense and contemporary romance, and urban fantasy under her penname, J.C. Daniels. You can find her at Twitter or Facebook. Read more about her work at her website. Sign up for her newsletter and have a chance to win a monthly giveaway.

www.shilohwalker.com

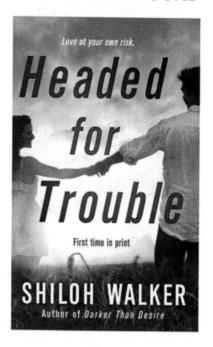

SHE'S A SMALL-TOWN GIRL WITH BIG DREAMS.

Nine years ago, Neve McKay fled her small Southern town and disapproving family to seek a career in the big city. Now she's finally coming home-and hoping for a fresh start. But the relationship that shattered her world still haunts her. And even among her nearest and dearest, she doesn't feel safe…

CAN THIS BAD BOY BE THE ANSWER TO HER PRAYERS?

Ian Campbell is a pure Scottish muscle-as hard and handsome as they come. But when Neve walks into his bar, his heart melts…and he vows to have this gorgeous and somewhat vulnerable woman in his life-for better or for worse. What is Neve's tragic secret? And how can Neve expect Ian to protect her, when doing so could put his own life at risk? The only thing Ian knows for sure is that he will do whatever it takes to keep her out of harm's way-and in his loving arms…

www.shilohwalker.com

YOU OWN ME

It had always been her…

Ten years had passed since the doors slammed shut behind Decker Calhoun, taking away his freedom, but more importantly, locking him away from Elizabeth Waters, the only woman he'd ever loved—the woman he'd given up everything for. The day he was sentenced, he'd looked at her and said, No regrets, Lizzie.

But he lied, because he did have one. Although he's been out of jail for three years now, he was a year too late. Lizzie never knew how he felt and just months before he was released, she found somebody else and it's too late.

Or maybe not. It seems that Lizzie's boyfriend wants an open relationship and two can play at that game. Now all Decker has to do is convince Lizzie that he's the better man…and has been all along.

www.shilohwalker.com